Those Who Whisper

R SULLINS

Copyright © 2023 by NEA Ink, LLC

All rights reserved.

No part of this book may be reproduced in any form or by any electronic or mechanical means, including information storage and retrieval systems, without written permission from the author, except for the use of brief quotations in a book review.

Edited by **Book Witch Author Services**

Cover by **JODIELOCKS Designs**

Floral cover by **Artscandare Book Cover Design**

Ingram Spark ISBN 979-8-9879214-2-5

Amazon ISBN 9798379326098

THOSE WHO WHISPER

···ARE LIKELY DEAD···

R. Sullins
PARANORMAL · CONTEMPORARY · ROMANCE

Introduction

I never expected to fall in love with a ghost...

I had to get away from my life.
As if anxiety was something I could escape from.
But landing a job half a world away,
teaching a precious little girl at her home in Scotland,
seemed like the perfect answer.
The Manor was beautiful.
Large and mysterious,
it held secrets that lurked
behind the glass panes and painted walls.
Secrets about a *witch*.
Secrets about a *curse*.
Secrets like - *all the ghosts from the past are still here.*
And they wanted **me** to end the curse.

But if I did, I would lose *him*.

Foreword

Who doesn't love to snuggle up with a ghost on those cold, rainy nights?

THIS IS A LITTLE DIFFERENT FROM WHAT I'VE WRITTEN IN THE PAST. I HOPE YOU ENJOY LACEY AND IAN'S STORY. FOR A FULL LIST OF CW/TW BEFORE READING CLICK HERE

One

Anxiety lived like an insidious snake inside my belly. Sometimes it slithered, writhing, keeping me just on the edge of a panic attack. Other times, it was curled up, content to sit back, one eye open, waiting for the perfect moment to strike. But always, always, it was ready to strike.

My anxiety was the compass to many of my decisions in life, including the one I had made two short weeks ago. Now, at the end of my fifteen-hour flight with three layovers, on a journey constantly surrounded by strangers, it was definitely no longer content to curl up and wait for a better time to strike. It was wound tightly like a coil, just waiting to break free. I was doing everything I could, practicing every technique my therapist had taught me, trying to get it to just *wait*.

When I was a kid, it wasn't so bad. It wasn't until I was around twelve years old that it began to slither its way into my body, ultimately taking up permanent residence. Eventually, my anxiety became so bad that my parents had to pull me out of school and home-teach me. It was easy enough for them to do, seeing as they were both college professors. With their influence and little to no outside interference from friends or any of the normal distractions of youth, I was able to graduate an entire year early from high school. Though my graduation consisted of a letter of congratulations and a diploma from the school I would have graduated from.

College was a completely awful experience, but by then, I had been taught several coping techniques that helped me enough to get through my days while surrounded by complete strangers. I was always a mess at the end of the day, but I made it through... usually.

So, knowing everything I did about my triggers—crowds of people being the biggest and worst, I had to ask myself repeatedly, why the *hell* I had decided I could be an elementary school teacher. I suppose I had assumed that young children wouldn't trigger an attack. Children were small, gentle, docile. It wouldn't possibly be like when I was surrounded by unknown adults. Oh, how dreadfully wrong I was.

The first day of 1st grade was such a disaster that I knew I would never be hired on at another school ever again. Lucky for me, I had already decided I wouldn't be trying.

And that *is* how I ended up on this epically long flight to Scotland.

I'd hugged my mother and placed a kiss on my father's bristly cheek before climbing into the back of an Uber. I had to promise my mother so many times that I would continue to practice my coping techniques so many times, it nearly threw me into another panic attack. I had agreed softly when she reminded me to get enough sleep each night and softly whispered to her when she started to explain how to handle an incoming attack, "I'll be okay, mom. I love you, too."

And now, here I was, somewhere over the Atlantic, off to a place I'd never been to, to live and work for people I had only spoken to a few times. I could feel the serpentine movements of my anxiety coiling around my insides as if stretching for its journey to the surface. I knew it was only a matter of time before it was released. I was sitting stiffly in my seat, looking out the small window, on the last leg of my journey. As I stared out the window and watched as the squares below grew larger and more recognizable as actual buildings instead of just indiscernible blobs, I wondered, again, just what in the hell I was thinking.

I started taking deeper breaths, inhaling the stale air of the plane. Leaning my head back against the seat, I closed my eyes in an attempt to find relief.

"Finger... wrist... elbow..." I tapped each place as I repeated the words. "Finger... wrist... elbow..." I opened my eyes and looked back out the window. "Water... trees... buildings..."

As my breathing slowed, I squeezed my eyes shut tight, taking in several slow inhales and exhales before nearly jumping out of my seat when the person next to me put their hand over mine, where I was still tapping on my wrist.

I swung my startled gaze over to the large, portly man that had taken up the majority of the seats in our row since we left JFK International. I watched as his lips moved, a smile on his face, then looked down at where his sweaty hand was still sitting on my skin. I looked back up at him before reluctantly tugging one of my earbuds free.

"I'm sorry, what?" I asked in a quiet voice. What I really wanted to say was to *get your hand off of me*, but anxiety didn't do you any favors when it was time to speak up for yourself to a stranger.

"I asked if you have plans for dinner?" His smile was hopeful, his slightly crooked teeth on full display. He may have been the nicest man on the planet, but I wasn't the kind of person that could spend any amount of time with a stranger and be okay in the end. It was unlikely that I would even be able to make it to the appetizer stage of a meal.

I slowly slid my arm out from under his hand, resisting the urge to pull out my bottle of hand sanitizer and dump it over my arm. "Ummm, no, I'm sorry. My family is waiting on me." It was absolutely true. The family that I was making this trip for was waiting on me.

I watched as his smile slid off his face like an ice cream melting off a cone in the middle of August. His smile returned after a few seconds, but it had changed. It was no longer hopeful and friendly.

"Well, perhaps you could use a ride then." He looked me up and down, huddled in my hoodie and yoga pants, comfort wear for such a long journey, before looking back up to meet my eyes and licking his lips. I couldn't take my eyes off the wetness gleaming there in the dull glow from the overhead lighting of the plane cabin. I shuddered. "American, right? I can show you around. Show you real Scottish hospitality."

I was already shaking my head before he was done speaking. "No, thank you, sir. I have a ride waiting for me at the airport and a very long drive." My manners necessitated that I tack on another, "Thank you, though." Even though I was most definitely not thankful.

He huffed and placed his arm on the armrest between our seats, effectively taking over half the space I had and digging his elbow into my arm without another word. All I could do was attempt to lean over toward the window as much as possible, but I had already been as curled into myself since the beginning of the flight as I could. Until now, he hadn't tried to invade more of my space than his girth required, but I had obviously pissed him off enough not to care anymore.

I put my earbud back in and turned back to look out the window, letting out a sigh of relief to see how much closer we were to the city of Edinburgh. Even through my music, I could hear the announcement that we were approaching our destination. All around me, people began to move, adjusting their seats and gathering their items while the flight attendants walked through with garbage bags.

Deep inside me, warring emotions fought. I was nervous, but it was an excited type of nervousness. I felt as if something major was going to happen. Something in this country was going to change the rest of my life. Adding to the constricting feeling inside me, I wasn't sure if it was going to change for the better or not, and that scared me.

Finally, with a jerk, the plane landed, and my body was thrown back against the seat. I closed my eyes at the sensation, breathing deeply to control my racing heart. This was happening so fast after so many hours of just sitting and waiting. My body was tense, and my mind was uncertain about the next step once the plane came to a stop. I would finally be on solid ground, and there would be no going back now. There would be a long car ride to the northern part of the country, but my journey was almost over.

I waited until nearly every person had stood up and was making their way down the aisle before I finally stood. I was thankful that the man beside me was one of the first to jump from his seat, obviously eager to leave. Picking up my backpack from the floor beneath my feet, I pulled it over my shoulder, then reached up to tug my carry-on bag from the overhead compartment.

I nodded my thanks to the flight attendant at the door and took in a huge lungful of the fresh air as soon as I made it onto the skybridge. Breathing in stale, recycled air for hours wasn't pleasant. I fervently hoped that this new position worked out well because I had no desire to go through the experience of the last day again anytime soon.

I walked quickly to the baggage claim after a fairly brief stop through passport control while keeping my head down and avoiding any eye contact with fellow travelers. Avoiding eye contact was something I had done for as long as I could remember and was usually a sure way to keep any strangers from attempting to strike up a conversation that had the potential to make me freak out. My dad said I put off a *fuck off* vibe, and I was perfectly okay with that.

The luggage from my flight was just beginning to make its rounds around the conveyor belt when I arrived, so I stood back and waited for the frenzy to die down as everyone descended on their colorful luggage, yanking it off the traveling belt, bumping into each other and talking loudly. For someone like me, it was a walking nightmare.

Finally, there were only a few bags left, so I stepped away from my waiting spot against the wall and carefully took the handle of my large suitcase, trying not to lose my balance when the weight almost took me with it as it tried to keep going. A hand joined mine on the handle and pulled hard, lifting the bag up and off before placing it gently onto the floor.

I glanced up through my lashes to see a woman a little older than me with dark hair and kind, green eyes smiling at me. Her accent was thick when she wished me a good day and a welcome to Scotland before walking away without even waiting for a thank you. My face was flaming in embarrassment, and I was cursing my awkwardness for the millionth time in my life as I pulled my suitcase along behind me on my way to customs.

By the time I was finished with the formalities of entering a new country, I was just about done. I had reached my limit. I needed space from the crowds of people, the noise, the *energy*. It was too much, and I had to blink several times, pushing it down, trying to hold back the flood that was threatening to escape as I walked toward the exit. I needed a quiet place to settle my nerves before I flew into a full-blown panic attack. The only problem was that I knew there was a driver waiting for me. If I could just reach the car, I could hide there, fixing myself before I reached my new employer's home. I would be okay by the time we reached that destination. I had to be.

I had explained my condition as a matter of full disclosure before I could accept the job offer. I couldn't in good conscience take care of someone's child without them being aware of my potential reactions to overstimulation. She had assured me repeatedly that she understood and was not overly worried. She had even gone as far as to assure me that her daughter could be an asset to me if I had an attack. It bothered me deeply that I could potentially place a little girl in that position, but I had hope that my therapy and coping mechanisms would keep that from happening. But this blackness that was creeping in around my vision was making me rethink everything.

My breathing was coming quicker, and I was about to find the nearest restroom so I could hide in a stall and cry out my frustration when I heard my name called out. I looked around to see an older gentleman with gray hair and a kind smile holding a sign with my name on it. A relieved tear slid down my cheek that I quickly swept away.

I ignored his concerned gaze as I pulled my heavy suitcase over to him and looked up. "I'm Lacey Conrad." If he noticed how shaky my voice was, he was polite enough to ignore it.

"Aye, Miss. Been a long journey for you. Let's get you to the Manor." He reached out for my suitcase but was observant enough to notice the death grip I had on the backpack I was using as an anchor at the moment. I was thankful he didn't try to take it from me as well.

All I could do was nod and whisper while looking back down at the floor. "Yes, please. Thank you so much."

With a relieved sigh, once we made it out of the crowd and to the car, I settled into the backseat of the sedan and closed my eyes. I let the gentle rocking of the car lull me to sleep.

Two

I jerked awake and started looking around, confused, not knowing what had woken me. Taking in my surroundings, the rocky hills and grass outside the car windows had me blinking in confusion until the last couple of days started coming back to me. I sat up straighter and paid closer attention to where we were.

We were just reaching a small town that had an old-world vibe, nothing like what I had ever seen in the United States. It was lovely, with cobblestone streets and colorful buildings. There were a few people walking and several children out playing with a dog on a side street as we passed. I fell in love in an instant, but it seemed as if I blinked, and the town was already behind us, and we were driving toward the ruins of an old castle.

My mouth dropped open at the amazing sight of the straight, square walls that still stood proud and tall in the sky. I couldn't take my eyes off them as we drew nearer. Much of the walls that were still standing were patchy with green moss. Even with the rocks crumbling around the base from age and weather, it was still one of the most wonderful sights I had ever seen in my life.

"It's a right beauty then, isn't it?" My driver asked, pulling me away from my awed staring.

I forgot to be shy and anxious when I turned to him, a huge smile on my face. "It's gorgeous! I've never seen anything like it before in my life!"

"Yer, in luck there, Miss. It's a great place to explore, long as yer careful and mind yer steps." He winked at me knowingly in the rearview mirror, and I looked down at my hands, but I couldn't keep my eyes away from the castle ruins.

"I can really go exploring there?"

"Aye."

I looked back up to thank him, but finally saw where we had been heading. The castle was impressive in its aged, formidable glory, but the building we were driving up to was every inch its modern counterpart. It couldn't necessarily be considered a castle, but it was certainly beyond being just a sprawling mansion.

I gasped and leaned forward as if I could get a better view. "She told me the house was called Moreland Manor, but… I never expected this."

He didn't say a word; he just chuckled as he drove past a pond with a fountain that was in the middle of the two-way lane before swinging the car around to park right in front of the massive double doors that looked to be an intimidating fifteen feet tall.

I was too shocked to get out of the car, my body suddenly feeling numb and immobile, so I was still sitting there staring when he came around and opened my door for me. He had to take my elbow and help me step out. I finally tore my eyes away from the building that I couldn't bring myself to call a house. "I don't think I can do this," I whispered, more to myself than to my driver.

I blinked and then blinked again when the old man threw his head back and laughed like I had said the funniest joke in the world. Here I was, standing in a day-old hoodie and yoga pants, in front of a freaking mansion that other mansions would be jealous of, and he was laughing at me. I crossed my arms and shuffled my feet while scowling.

When he was done, he wiped his eyes with the sleeve of his cream-colored cable-knit sweater, still chuckling. "Aye, Miss. Yer, gonna be fine."

I looked back up at the place. It was too big to truly take in. It was gray brick with so many pointed peaks and balconies I couldn't count them all. They had flowers flowing over them, softening the serious edges and giving it a lovely quality. But the colorful flowers couldn't disguise the faintly menacing feeling, nor did they chase away the chill I felt when I took in the reflecting light of the windowpanes. It was as if the house itself was somehow warning me to stay away. That the outside was safer than the inside.

"Ye ready, Miss?"

The sound of my suitcase being dropped to the ground and being rolled toward the massive doors shook me out of my musings, and I rubbed my arms to chase away the chill that crept over me. I quickly reached back into the open car door to grab my backpack and pulled a strap over my shoulder, and chased after the man. I really should have asked for his name. My mother would have been so disappointed in me.

I caught him at the door, my short legs no match for his long strides. "Excuse me, sir? I wanted to say thank you for the ride. And... to ask you for your name?" My face heated with embarrassment, and I looked down at the cuff of my sleeve, picking at invisible lint.

"'Tis Doogal, Miss. Given name is Douglas, but been called Doogal since I was a wee lad." He tipped his head with a smile. "Always at yer service." At that, he opened the giant door with surprisingly little effort, and I braced myself for what the inside would look like.

What I *hadn't* braced myself for was how stepping across the threshold would make me feel.

Warmth bathed my insides. It was like the time I drank a cup of coffee mixed with Irish cream liquor; I felt soothed and comforted all at once. I felt like I was walking into *home*. The house seemed to open up and welcome me in, as if it had been waiting for me to arrive. My heart felt happy and full, and I was sure that I was truly at peace for the first time in my life.

I spun around in a circle slowly, with eyes as wide as saucers, as I took in the interior of the Manor. The entry led into one large open space that was as long as a football field and half as wide. The marble floors gleamed brightly, and no speck of dirt seemed to dare fall onto the white and gray surface.

Several doors spaced widely on the left side showed rooms on that side of the Manor, but on the right side were two open spaces where large hallways led to who knew where. So far, everything in the place was proving to be huge. If it weren't for so much white, though, it would have been fairly gloomy since there were very few light fixtures, and I couldn't help a shiver as I wondered how dark it would get at night.

There were several stairways leading to the second floor, and each had gleaming newel posts that matched the molding along the walls. The whole place was an interior designer's dream, and it was done beautifully and tastefully. Whoever was responsible for it should be rewarded, and likely was.

Clicking footsteps tore me from my intense perusal of the great hall, making my eyes dart to the owner of the sound. I straightened my shoulders and subconsciously began smoothing my clothing, trying to appear as well put together as was possible, given the circumstances.

"Lacey! I'm so glad you made it!"

Isla McMillan, my new employer, was striding towards me in a beautiful dress with shiny nude heels and a full face of makeup, making her look like the ideal model for business women everywhere. She was a tall woman made even taller in those heels, but she was also extremely beautiful with strawberry blonde hair and green eyes. I couldn't help but be envious of her innate grace and beauty. She put her hands on my forearms and gave them a light squeeze, giving me a quick once-over.

"You look well. The trip must have been horrid." She turned toward Doogal with a smile. "Doogal, dear, could you take Lacey's bags to her room? You know which one? Thank you so much for fetching her. Make sure you take the day off tomorrow for your trouble."

"Ne'er mind all that now. It was nothing but a drive any fool could do." He was already moving off towards the nearest staircase, waving off Isla's words, done with the conversation.

She hooked her elbow with mine, and I had a quick stab of tension before letting my shoulders relax. I allowed her to lead me down the long hall as she explained which rooms were beyond the doors to our left. I had to concentrate on my breathing for several minutes until I had settled enough to nod and engage with her. I knew that the first two doors concealed a parlor and a study, but when we reached the library, I was fully invested.

"Is that somewhere I will have access?" I couldn't help but ask.

She looked at me strangely as we walked past the closed double doors. "Lacey, you are welcome to go anywhere. This is your home now, too. I know you will be working for me, but despite how it looks, this isn't like one of those super strict, stuck-up, posh places." She shuddered. "I might have grown up in this monstrosity, but my mama would have whipped mine and my brother's bums if we'd acted too good for anyone else."

I couldn't help but giggle quietly. She was hard to hold back from. Her personality was just so warm and open. My complete opposite in every way. How strange that I should feel so comfortable around her, then.

"I didn't know you had a brother. Does he live somewhere else?"

Her face fell, and she sniffed delicately. "He is... no longer with us."

"I'm so sorry! I didn't know!"

She waved a hand dismissively and gave a watery smile. "How could you? I never spoke of him during our video chats. It's still very fresh." She gave a harsh, short laugh. "I may be a McMillan now, but I will always be a Campbell, and us Campbells are used to tragedy. I'm sure you will learn that sooner than later." She shook her head and led me into a warm and cheery kitchen and over to a small rectangular table that was out of place in the rest of the Manor. It was worn, scratched, and scuffed. Well-loved. A witness to countless cups of tea and stories across generations.

She directed me to sit down as she got a teakettle on to heat and sat down across from me, crossing her arms. "Forgive me. It's been a stressful time lately." She stared at the table and blew out a long breath before looking up at me with a bright smile pasted on her face. "What about you? Tell me all about your trip."

My eyes darted around the room at being put on the spot, at needing to talk about myself, and I gripped my leg hard to ground myself. I closed my eyes for a quick second, then opened them again, forcing myself to look Isla in the eye. "I used my headphones a lot to keep from having to talk to people. Halfway through the trip, they died, so I had to pretend they were working, but luckily, on my last layover out of JFK airport, I was able to charge them again. I was careful to use them sparingly on the flight here."

When I stopped talking, I blinked at her as she stared at me with wide eyes. Finally, the tension broke, and we both fell into giggles. "I'm so sorry, Isla. You must think I'm a mess. I promise I'm usually not as bad as I've been today. It's mostly because I'm tired and stressed out from traveling and the crowds. When I'm in a usual routine, I'm almost normal."

Her face got fierce, losing the mirth she'd had just a moment ago. She reached across the table, grabbing my hand and squeezing, just shy of painful. "Now, you listen to me, Lacey Conrad! There is nothing wrong with you! Everyone has a quirk or two. Some people are a little more special than others, and some may need a softer touch than someone else. But not one single person has anything *wrong* with them. You take care of yourself. You use the techniques that help you make it through the day. And you don't explain yourself to anyone. Ever. Understand?"

I stared at her as she fumed and blinked back tears of her own. I knew why she was so fierce in her protection of anyone with special needs, and I couldn't help but appreciate her words. My parents loved and supported me, but they hadn't been the champion that Isla was.

The teakettle started screaming just as I opened my mouth to say something, to tell her that I appreciated her words. Instead, she jumped out of her seat as if she had been jolted and rushed over to turn it off. I sat there looking at the scratched table top as I heard the clinking of teacups and saucers.

Isla set down a beautifully dressed tray with floral printed china. She handed me a cup with an apologetic smile. It was my turn to wave away any apology. It was a long 24 hours for me and several rough years for her. We were both entitled to have emotional outbursts.

When she brought out cookies that she called shorties to eat with our tea, I groaned in pleasure at how wonderful they tasted. There was a lot I was going to have to get used to here. Having moved to a whole other country with different customs and ways of doing everyday things, not to mention simple things like food. But I was determined to do my best to acclimate, and I wanted to enjoy doing so.

We sat there and had our tea with much more pleasant conversation once we both settled in and became comfortable with each other. She told me all about the quaint village that we had passed through and the ruins that she and her brother used to play hide and seek in when they were children. What she didn't do was tell me anything about the curse that had been hovering over her family for nearly 200 years.

Three

A sweet giggle echoed through the great hall and bounced to us through the open doorway of what Isla had explained to me was the family kitchen. Long ago, Isla's grandmother had decided she didn't like being waited on hand and foot. She hadn't been brought up in the aristocracy. After just a few weeks of having her every need met, and being absolutely miserable, she had put her foot down and demanded her own kitchen space and a family dining area.

From there, this warm, welcoming space was born. With a wood-burning stove at one end to keep the draft out and a modern stove at the other. The table we were sitting at was the very same one gifted to her grandmother by her husband all those years ago. All the children since then have found themselves sitting at it to do their schoolwork instead of in the study where it used to be done. It had become the heart of the home.

The most precious little girl walked in slowly, with curly red hair and freckles dancing across her nose and cheeks. Her green eyes were sparkling with happiness when she spotted her mother. "Mam!" She threw herself forward, crutches and all. Isla dodged them with years of experience and love.

Olivia caught sight of me when she lifted her head from her mother's embrace and yelled out a happy, "Lacey! You're here!" She quickly made her way around the table and gave me a hug similar to the way she had held her mam. I did my best to copy Isla's movements to avoid the elbow crutches as I wrapped my arms around her tiny shoulders.

"Olivia, sweetheart. I'm so happy to see you in person finally! You are even lovelier than you were over the screen of my laptop." I tapped the tip of my finger against her button nose as she giggled sweetly.

Olivia was my new student and the reason I had been hired and then flown halfway across the world. I had fallen in love with the child over several video chats, as we had gotten to know each other before the decision was made that we would all take the chance for me to come all the way out here. But, seeing her in the flesh, meeting her mother, and being in this home, I knew I had made the right choice.

"Olivia, love, are you ready for bedtime?" Isla asked her softly.

"Yes, mam. I came to say goodnight. Miss Chasity said you were too busy to come up to me." I didn't miss the quick glare that Isla shot the nurse who hovered in the doorway with her hands folded in front of her. But, when she looked back at her daughter, the look was nothing but patient and loving.

"Olivia, darling, I am never too busy for you. Shall I tuck you in?" She stood, already prepared to lead her daughter to her room.

Olivia walked slowly, the braces on her legs preventing her from going much quicker than she already was, back towards Isla. "Yes, please! Will you read to me?"

"Of course, darling." Isla looked up at me with an apologetic smile. "I'm sure you must be exhausted yourself, Lacey. I'll have Chasity show you to your room so you can get settled and maybe have a nice, relaxing bath. After a long trip, I know I like to indulge in a long soak before resting."

I stood up as well, the exhaustion I had been pushing back since I arrived at the house starting to settle more heavily on my shoulders. "A hot bath sounds wonderful, to be honest." I turned to Olivia and bent down to her short six-year-old level. "I'll see you in the morning, sweetheart. You have a good rest, okay?"

"Yes, Lacey!" She gave me a big smile that warmed my heart and then left with Isla.

I turned to face the nurse, who gave me a short, curt nod and turned in a different direction. "Miss Olivia has an elevator near her room. For obvious reasons."

"Yes," I murmured. "For obvious reasons."

Not waiting for me, she walked ahead, leading me to a set of stairs. Our footsteps echoed in the great hall as we moved through it. It was something I would need to get used to. It was definitely darker than it had been earlier when I had arrived. I looked up and noticed the skylights that covered the length of the room. They were enough to light the hall during the day, but now that the sun was setting low, the lamps that lit the hall were barely adequate to illuminate the large space.

The stairs were also made of marble but were lined with a plush carpet runner that my feet sunk into as we ascended toward the second floor. Once we reached the landing, there were additional choices to make. We could follow the railing lining the great hall or take one of the hallways leading to the bedrooms. Chasity led me down the center hallway, and my door was at the very end.

The nurse bobbed her head without turning the knob, leaving without saying a word. I ignored her standoffish attitude and reached for the crystal knob. It was warmer than I had anticipated it to be when I placed my hand on it.

The room was just as large and elaborate as one would expect of a manor of this magnitude. I could easily fit four of my apartments from the States in this one room. It was done in beautiful, soft teal colors, and I loved it immediately.

The bed was made of dark wood carved with elaborate scenes of cherubs dancing, making me smile. Sheer teal curtains were hanging from the tall posters in each corner. The walls were covered in pearlescent damask wallpaper, and there was a matching wardrobe and desk. A comfortable-looking chair sat in one corner.

I laughed softly and hugged myself. I felt like a princess standing in such a fantastic room.

Remembering that I needed to call my parents, I dug through my backpack and found my phone with just enough battery to make a quick call to let them know that I had made it to my destination okay. I had to assure them that Isla and Olivia were just as lovely as they had seemed over the video calls. Maybe even more so. I had to promise to call again soon before my mom would finally allow me to hang up. I hadn't thought I would miss them as much as I did, and I wiped a stray tear that fell when I looked down at my quiet phone. I found my charger, plugged it into the wall next to the bed, then set the alarm for the next morning. I knew if I didn't, I would probably oversleep due to the time change. It was going to be a rough few days as I acclimated.

Exploring the room, I walked to the open door and saw an ensuite bathroom with an old-fashioned clawfoot tub with gleaming gold feet and handles. I immediately went over to it and turned on the hot water, groaning when steam began to pour out of the tap almost immediately. I plugged the drain before walking back into the bedroom to look for my luggage.

I didn't see it out in the open, but a quick glance in the wardrobe showed me that someone had unpacked for me, and my cheeks grew hot. I hoped Doogal wasn't the one to do it. Someone had touched my bras and panties, but I couldn't imagine it would have been the old man, though.

I took a cotton nightgown from the drawer and walked back into the bathroom, placing the gown on top of the white countertop. Trying to familiarize myself with the space, I searched around the white and immaculately clean bathroom, opening a few drawers to see it was fully stocked with all the necessities a woman would need. I pulled my dark hair up into a twist, secured it with a hair tie I procured from a drawer, and looked at my reflection in the mirror. Noting the bags under my eyes. My blue eyes were usually bright, but even I could see that they looked dull and tired. I glanced down to grab a toothbrush and toothpaste, placing a small amount on the bristles before running it under the tap to wet.

When I brought it up to my mouth to begin brushing, I looked back at myself again in the mirror and let out a horrified gasp. The brush dropped from my hand, clattering into the sink basin. Spinning around, my heart racing frantically, I blinked several times at the empty room in front of me and beyond into the bedroom. I was completely alone. So why did I see someone standing in the mirror behind me? I shook my head. It had to have been a trick of the light. Maybe it was the steam from the bath. I was exhausted, and the house had my imagination in overdrive.

I glanced over at the bathtub, rushed over to turn the tap off, tested the temperature, and pulled my hand away with a gasp at the icy feel of the water. I was so sure I had turned on the hot water. How was it possible that it was so cold? I didn't believe that a house like this would not have a water heater large enough to fill a tub before going cold.

I shook my head, pulled the stopper up to drain the tub, and went back to the sink. I started cursing at the mess I made of the toothpaste when the brush had fallen into the sink. Toothpaste was smeared on the once pristine, white sink in several places. I quickly rinsed the mess away and finished brushing my teeth. By the time I was done, the tub had finished draining. This time, I got stripped out of my clothes as it was filling and watched it the whole time. The steam rose, making my body sag with the need for the soothing warmth it would provide. I dipped a toe in gingerly, letting out a slight hiss at the heat.

I climbed into the hot water and let it fill up to the top of my chest, indulging in such a deep soak. I had never had a tub I could fill so full before. Usually, the tubs I had were less than satisfying, being too small to really relax in and could barely fill up to my sides. With a groan, I relaxed fully into the hot, soothing water, letting my neck rest against the rolled lip of the tub.

I must have dozed off because the next thing I knew, my head was completely under the water, and I was struggling to pull myself back up, but my hands kept slipping against the sides. Grasping for purchase, I started to panic. Someone had their hands on the top of my head and was holding me under. I screamed in terror, fighting to get up and thrashing around in the water. Water was sloshing all over the place, cascading over the sides of the tub, likely soaking the floor, but try as I might, I couldn't pull myself up.

Suddenly, the pressure on my head was gone, and I shot up out of the water with a gasp of air filling my lungs and immediately began coughing. Pushing my wet hair out of my eyes, I looked around wildly to find what or who had held me down. I could feel my heart beating an erratic rhythm, with terror clogging my veins. My pulse was echoing loudly in my ears. Then, just like when I thought I saw a face behind me in the mirror, I could have sworn I saw a man's face near the door before it faded into nothingness.

I jumped out of the tub, slipped on the water all over the floor, and sprawled naked, still coughing and gasping. Trying to still my frantic mind and catch my breath.

"What. The. Fuck?!" That did *not* just happen. *I had not been nearly drowned by a ghost.*

I slipped and slid to my feet, grabbed a neatly folded towel off the rack, and wrapped it around my body. My hands were shaking so badly I could barely tuck the end at my breasts. I ran a hand over my soaking wet hair, pulling back the strands that were stuck to my cheeks, and looked at the mess.

"How am I supposed to explain this?" I muttered between coughing fits. Then, finally, I shook my head, grabbed every towel I could find, and dropped them all on the floor to soak up the water. I would have to apologize to the housekeeper in the morning.

I glanced at the shower, but shook my head again. There was no way I was taking a shower right then. I could just wait until the morning to wash and brush the tangles out of my hair. I needed to calm my nerves first before I placed myself in another vulnerable position.

Snagging my nightgown off the counter, I walked back into the bedroom, closing the door behind me. I was done for the night. I'd had too much anxiety for one day, and it was finally getting the best of me. I was too tired to deal with any more.

I pulled the towel off and dried my hair as well as I could before draping it over the doorknob on the bathroom door, not wanting to go back in to hang it properly, then slipped the gown over my head. Sliding back the gorgeous bedding, I crawled into the middle of the bed and slipped inside the sheets. I wasn't too tired to appreciate the luxurious feel of them against my skin.

I thought after the long day and the scare in the bathroom, I would have been able to drop into a deep sleep. But instead, I tossed and turned, eventually falling into a restless sleep haunted by a handsome face that faded before I could get a close look at who it was. Or ask him why he had tried to kill me.

Four

I sat straight up in bed, my hand over my heart and breathing hard as if I had been running from the devil. I thought back to the dream I'd been having and figured that analogy wasn't too far off.

I reached over to grab my phone to turn off the alarm. With a groan, I stared at the time and dropped back onto my pillow, and stared at the teal canopy above me. The dream I'd been having was beginning to feel hazy, like it was morning mist being burned away by the first rays of the sun. As hard as I tried to remember what had made me so frightened when I'd first woken up, I just couldn't.

I looked over toward the closest window, but I couldn't see anything through the curtains. I let out a pitiful whine before finally giving up and rising, swinging my legs over the side of the bed. The carpet was thick and soft, but it was still chilly. I would have to pick up a pair of slippers soon. It was a good excuse to visit the tiny village, even if the thought had my heart rate picking up.

I finally stopped procrastinating and made my way to the closed bathroom door, taking the towel off the knob before placing my hand on it and swallowing hard. I cracked it open and peeked in, not really knowing what I expected to see, but it was exactly as I had left it last night.

Wet towels littered the floor, and I swung the door open the rest of the way with a weary sigh. I began picking up the heavy towels, still weighed down from their soaking the previous night, and dropped them into the tub with a wet plop. What had felt excessive before, I was now relieved had been heavily stocked in the first place.

Once I had the floor cleared, I placed the towel I had used the night before on the hook by the shower and reached inside the spacious stall to turn on the water. I wasn't ashamed to say that I glanced around nervously before actually stepping inside and putting my head under the spray. I had seen my fair share of horror films, and they rarely ended well for the girl in the shower.

I was rinsing the shampoo from my hair when I heard it. Indistinct voices that I tried to ignore as a figment of my imagination. But when there was a sudden, high-pitched and fury-filled scream right next to my ear, I opened my eyes wide, forgetting about the shampoo that was still there.

I frantically splashed water into my face and rubbed to get the sting to dissipate, then reached with shaky hands to shut off the water.

"Who's there?" My voice was trembling as badly as my knees as I called out to the empty room. There was no one with me, and no way someone could have left that quickly without a sound. I sagged against the tiled wall. Surely, I was losing my mind, or Isla had left out some very important information when she had hired me. Like her house being haunted. That's the one word that kept bouncing through my brain. As much as my rational mind wanted to scoff and deny the very possibility, it made the most sense.

I finished my shower quickly and didn't bother drying my hair past running the towel over it briskly. I just threw it up into a bun as I got ready to leave my room. I needed answers, and I needed the Lady of the Manor to give them to me.

I was down the stairs and walking into the kitchen just a few minutes after the incident. I came to a stop in the doorway, the scene bringing a genuine smile to my face and a warmth to bloom inside me. Isla and Olivia were sitting close together, their heads bent over a coloring book, somehow able to share the same page without getting in each other's way. That was something I wanted one day. The bond with a child that only a parent had.

Isla looked up with a smile at my approach, but her face dropped when she took in my appearance. "Oh, dear."

I grunted and pulled out the same chair I had sat in the night before, crossing my arms on the table in front of me. And waited. Olivia looked up and gave me her bright smile, helping to chase away so much of the lingering terror that had been clinging to me.

She held up her coloring book, making several crayons go rolling in different directions. "Lacey! Look what mam and me did!"

"Oh, sweetheart. It's lovely!" It truly was. The page was filled with flowers and kittens, and it was obvious that Olivia tried very hard to color between the lines. Though her choices of colors were typical of any six-year-old, her talent was outstanding. "Perhaps I can sweet talk you into making me a picture that I could hang in my bedroom?"

She turned her smile to her mother and bounced in her chair. "Oh! Did you hear? Lacey wants me to make her a picture!"

Isla ran a hand tenderly over her daughter's head and said, "I did, darling."

Olivia immediately started flipping through the pages until she found the one that she wanted and declared that it was going to be the one she colored for me.

Isla stood and took her time making me a cup of tea before finally setting it down in front of me, along with a plate of toast. It took me way too long to process what I was seeing and smelling. I looked up at Isla with so much gratitude it was embarrassing.

"Coffee?" I held the cup in both hands and took a sip without even taking the time to add milk and sugar. I glanced over to the counter behind her chair to spot a brand-new Keurig machine. How had I not smelled the rich aroma immediately?

She cleared her throat and stirred her own cup with more concentration than it warranted. "I'm not going to lie. It was to do something nice for the young woman that came halfway across the world to teach my daughter. But now, I think it's also turned into a bit of a bribe to stay?" She looked up at me with a pleading look.

I shook my head as I poured milk into my cup and added a couple of spoonfuls of sugar. I was stirring slowly to gather my thoughts before looking back at her. "I don't know what's happening, Isla."

She nodded and swallowed heavily, looking as if she were weighing her words carefully when Olivia cheerfully announced what we both were already thinking. "We have lots and lots of ghosts!" She never looked up from her coloring as she nonchalantly dropped the bomb on the room.

I looked back at Isla, and she gave me a weak smile. "In my defense, I had hoped you would never find out."

I raised an eyebrow and took a sip from my cup as I thought about the feeling of being held under the water. And the conclusion I had been desperately trying to deny.

"It's usually only family members that hear them. Sometimes a person that works here will see or hear something after they have been here for a very long time. They aren't usually active with newcomers. It's really only the mistresses that get the most..." she stopped and swallowed hard. I could have sworn she looked faintly green. "...activity."

"Mistresses?" I asked with a squeak, sitting back in my chair. Were there so many over the years? Was this normal? No, it couldn't be. I felt scandalized just thinking about it.

Isla looked at me, confused, until her face cleared, and she began laughing hard enough to make her eyes tear up. "Oh, dear. I needed that." She dabbed at her eyes delicately with the edge of a linen napkin as I wished for the floor to develop a hole to swallow me up. "The Mistress is the Lady of the Manor. Same as the Master is the Lord of the Manor." She finished with a chuckle.

I looked at her with confusion. "Aren't you the Lady of the Manor?"

She stared down at the table with a sigh and traced a heavily worn scratch with a fingertip. "I suppose so, but only in the strictest meaning. That role should have gone to my brother's wife. I never wanted it." She looked over at her daughter and smiled big, with a much cheerier tone. "Darling, it's time for your therapy. Miss Chasity is coming now to take you up. Are you finished?"

Olivia gave a small pout, but put her crayons away anyway. "I'm not done yet. But I'll be able to finish after my rest, won't I, mam?"

"Of course, darling. Go on up with Chasity. I will join you as soon as I talk to Lacey." She leaned over and tickled Olivia lightly. "Your schooling starts tomorrow, remember?"

"School! I'm so excited! I get to learn spelling and arim-, arib-"

"Arithmetic, sweet girl. We'll have you adding and subtracting your numbers in no time at all." I told her just as her nurse walked into the room in a similar outfit as yesterday of navy slacks, a blouse, and a cardigan. She was just a few years older than I was, but her cold demeanor made her seem much, much older. I hoped she was a good nurse to Olivia, if not less frosty.

Once they were gone, Isla turned back to me. "You need to tell me what you heard or saw, and I need to tell you the legend of the curse."

"You're serious?"

"My dear Lacey, we don't joke about the curse around here." She sat her teacup down with a small thump. "I'll begin by telling you the story of how it all started. That really explains it all, honestly." She cleared her throat and shifted in her seat. She seemed hesitant, but began, immediately absorbing me into the story with her words.

"Legend has it that the first Lord of Moreland Manor was in an arranged marriage, which was very common in those days. This was somewhere at the turn of the century between 1795 and 1800. The record-keeping those days could be a bit sketchy, and there was a fire in the records hall in the 1800's, so a lot of what records they did have were destroyed." She waved away her ramblings with a hand. "Anyway. They were married by arrangement and settled in here at the Manor. It was known by all that the Lady was not happy. She hated the cold winds that blew up from the ocean cliffs. She hated the isolation. She hated the very bricks the Manor was built from. And soon, that hate turned to her husband."

She took a sip of her tea and stared down into her cup. "It was during one of her rampages through the upstairs halls, where she would run and scream, terrorizing everyone into hiding, even her own son, that she caught her husband with his arms around a young servant girl. Now, some say he was simply trying to calm the girl because she was terrified of what the Lady was doing. Others said that he had been having an affair with the girl. Regardless, the Lady cursed them both before she pushed them out of a second-floor window."

I leaned forward when she finished speaking. That was not it. There had to be more to the story. I didn't do cliffhangers, damn it! "Well? What did she curse them with? What happened to her afterward? What happened with everyone else?"

She smiled, and I knew then I had been pulled right into her trap. "Well, she cursed her husband... and all future Lords, that they would die before they could have forever with their true love. And the servant girl that may or may not have been his mistress? Supposedly, she was pregnant. The Lady said that there could be no other Lady of the Manor but her."

I blinked. "That was it?"

"That was it. Her wrath was more for her husband, I suppose. Honestly, I don't blame her. Though her reaction was a little overboard, if you ask me."

I laughed, "A little? She's cursed every generation of your family since your great-great-great..."

"Four greats, if I'm not mistaken. Did I mention that shortly after she shoved her poor husband and the servant girl out the window to die of broken necks, she was accused of witchcraft?"

I scoffed. "Every woman back then that was even slightly different from the norm was accused of witchcraft.'

She nodded her head. "True, true. But weird things began to happen after her death. Mostly by her grandson, who had returned to the Manor after being sent far away to school, began hearing screams similar to the ones his grandmother used to make when she'd go into one of her fits. At first, people didn't believe him and started to say he was going as crazy as she had been. But, then the servants who had worked at the Manor the longest began hearing it too. And so it went on."

She stood up. "Would you like to see the Hall of Portraits? Each Lord of the Manor is painted there along with his Lady."

I stood up with her. "Of course."

The walk wasn't too long, but she did point out a few more rooms as we passed by, including a conservatory that was filled with gorgeous greenery that I couldn't wait to check out.

We turned down another hall, and she came to a stop. Unlike the great hall, this one was well lit, with wall sconces between each painting that was encased in glass, just like how you would see in a museum.

"My mother wanted to make sure the paintings were preserved as long as possible. She said the better protected now, the longer they can be on display here instead of being stored away later." She cleared her throat and spread her hands out, indicating the portraits on either side of the hall. "These are my grandparents. Every single one of them died within a few years of being married. Each one of them had a chance to have at least one boy child before meeting an untimely death somewhere on the estate."

She was walking as she spoke until she got down to the end of the portraits to one that didn't have a female beside it. She stood there in front of the frame and wiped a tear from her eye. I walked toward it slowly, as if drawn to it, unable to pull away. I couldn't have left the hall if I tried. But I didn't want to. My heart was as drawn to the man in that frame just as much as my body was physically.

When I finally reached the portrait and could see the man's handsome face properly, I swallowed hard. He had dark hair brushed away from his strong face. His square jaw gave him a stubborn look, and I felt like I was looking at a man that could easily have been a Highland warrior from hundreds of years in the past.

As I stared into the green eyes that seemed to be staring right into my soul, I asked through a thick lump in my throat. "Who is it?"

"My brother."

The face that had faded from my memory seconds after I had flung myself out of the tub last night had finally come back to me. I was looking at it through the glass.

Five

As much as I adored the little girl in front of me, I was relieved that our sessions were short. She was so sweet and a joy to teach. Olivia was eager to learn and soaked up knowledge like a sponge. But her needs as a six-year-old, as well as her physical needs, only allowed for short stretches of learning time.

We had just finished our morning lesson, and I watched as she was led away by the nurse, who seemed to at least show the proper amount of patience with the little girl as she slowly made her way out of the warm family kitchen and off to her rooms for her therapy session. After that, she would have her lunch and a nap before I was scheduled to meet with her again in the early afternoon.

Isla was gone for the day for her job at the local bank in town. I learned that when she wasn't working, she did her best to be a very hands-on mother. I didn't want to pry, but I could sense there was a sad story attached to whatever happened with Olivia's father. My heart went out to her. I couldn't imagine what that story was, but it must be difficult being a single parent. Even one with the kind of benefits that wealth provided.

I lay my head on my crossed arms and considered taking a quick nap. It had been another rough night, and one of the reasons I was guilty over being glad that my learning session with Olivia was over already. I had tossed and turned again in my comfortable bed with the luxurious sheets, unable to find sleep due to all the voices that wouldn't stop.

Over and over throughout the night, indistinct voices had continued to grow more and more urgent, seeming to echo around the room. Covering my head with the pillow hadn't helped at all, and it wasn't until I finally put my earbuds in with the music on as loud as I could handle it that I finally fell asleep. But then the dreams started. Just like the night before, the dreams evaporated the moment I woke up, but I was left with distinct impressions of others' pain and heartache weighing heavily on my mind, despite not remembering anything in great detail. I wish I knew whose emotions I was feeling and why. I couldn't help but wonder if I was dreaming about the story Isla had told me, my subconscious playing it like a movie in my mind. But I was more frightened of the possibility that my mind was warning me about something I couldn't grasp.

Always, my thoughts drifted back to the portrait of the last Lord of the Manor. Isla's brother, Ian, had been just twenty-eight when he died only a month ago. When Isla had spoken to me of him while we had our morning breakfast together, her grief was palpable. As she described the brother that she had lost, my heart ached for her. By all accounts, he seemed like he was such a good brother and uncle, opening the family home to them soon after Olivia was born, without a single question.

When I tentatively asked how he had died, she told of how he had fallen from his bedroom balcony.

"Honestly," she had said with tears in her eyes, "he should have survived the fall. There are shrubs under his balcony. It would have hurt, but not like it would have if he'd made an impact with the stone ground."

"I'm so sorry, Isla." I reached out to hold her trembling hand. "What happened, then?"

"He hit his head on the railing when he fell." She shook her head. "It never made sense, and I still don't understand it. There was no way that he could have just fallen. He hadn't been drinking to make him lose his balance. The investigation was marked as suspicious, but there was no evidence of foul play, so they closed the case quickly." She looked at me through watery lashes. "He didn't die until he reached the hospital. Since we are such a small town here, he needed to be flown. I was told that once he was in theatre, he died on the table."

Our conversation stalled when we heard the familiar tapping of crutches and little feet heading our way. Isla quickly dried her tears and composed herself. For the second morning in a row, I was welcomed with open arms to join their little family of two.

Still struggling with the time difference and lack of sleep, I decided that I needed some fresh air to clear my foggy mind. Grabbing my phone, earbuds, and a book, I stepped outside the Manor for the first time since I had arrived and headed out to explore the property.

Tilting my head back and inhaling deeply, I looked past the roof of the Manor, seeing nothing but the cloud filled sky, the sun hidden from my view. I took another deep breath and steadied myself, deciding to take the first path I found that seemed to lead toward the castle ruins. I could hear the faint crashing of waves far below the cliffs, even though I really wasn't close. Though I was tempted to get close enough to get a look at what sat below the edge, just the thought of being that close made heat prickle along my scalp and a shiver run down my spine. I had never considered myself scared of heights, but there were some inner alarm bells going off, telling me to stay far, far away from the cliffs.

I popped the earbuds in my ears and turned some music on low, tucking my phone into my pocket and shaking off the uneasy feeling. It was early fall, and I had been warned that the temperature was much lower than the average in the United States, but I hadn't quite expected it to be as chilly as it was. It was still in the eighties when I left Kentucky only a few days ago.

I had started out with my arms tight around me, trying to hold in the warmth from my hoodie, when I started to huff a little more than I had expected to. From a distance, the path had looked mostly flat, but now that I was close to halfway to the ruins, I found I was walking a slight but steady incline, and I was cursing all the skipped gym visits over the last year.

Finally, I came to the first of the fallen stones that were grown over with grass and moss. They were bigger than I had expected, and I carefully stepped around what I could and used my hands as leverage to climb past what I couldn't. Eventually, I made it past the outer edge and found myself in deep shadows as the tall rock walls stood several feet above me.

I stood in the middle of what would have been a very large room and spun around slowly, taking in the space and marveling at the size. I let my eyes drift close as I pictured what it would have looked like hundreds of years ago. I imagined a large man with dark hair hanging to his shoulders and bright eyes smoldering with the promise of something I hadn't experienced yet, but knew that I would in his arms. I tried to ignore that the face closely resembled the one in the portrait back at the Manor.

Sitting down on the mossy grass, I lay back with my hands on my chest and let in the fantasy of having a 17th-century Highlander wrap his strong arms around me. My dreams always tended to stall whenever I tried to imagine what it would be like to have a man touch me. I could never picture a face, and the faceless man that was reaching for me always tended to dissipate like smoke the moment we reached for each other.

This time, I could almost feel the heat of his skin as it brushed against mine, the puff of air stirring the strands of hair around my face as he leaned over me on the ground. The thought startled me back to reality and had my eyes flying open, a scream caught in my throat.

Ian Campbell's face hovered above me, his form just a wisp of a thought that looked like it would disappear if I waved a hand through it. I frantically scrambled back on my butt, scraping my palms against the small rocks hidden under the soft moss.

"P-please don't hurt me." I whimpered.

He was already moving back away from me as I spoke with his palms facing forward in a gesture that spoke of someone that was trying to indicate that he wouldn't cause me harm.

I swallowed and hunched forward, hugging my knees, and looked back the way I had come through the ruins, then toward him again. "Why did you try to drown me? Is it because of your family? I swear, I'm not here to hurt them! I'm just here to teach Olivia, that's all!"

He looked confused at my words, but shook his head and floated forward a pace. I leaned back, ready to bolt if I needed to. I may have thought he was the most handsome man I'd ever seen, but I wasn't eager to be murdered by any ghost—handsome or not. My reaction had him stopping and running a frustrated hand through his translucent hair.

It was almost comical. The entire situation was unreal. But my heart rate was racing out of control, and tears of fear were pricking my eyes. Suddenly, the once peaceful ruins felt terrifying and ominous.

But, as I thought about how scary it had turned, the air turned colder, and Ian Campbell's eyes grew sharper as they darted to the left. That was when I realized what I thought was scary was nothing, absolutely nothing, compared to the menacing figure that hovered several feet away, staring at the two of us.

She was old with stringy gray hair that waved in the air with wind I couldn't feel. She wore a period dress from the 1800s in all black that was ragged and torn. Her skin was as gray as her hair, and stretched tightly over the sharp bones of her cheeks. Her eyes were deep, pitch black pools. The evil that radiated from her froze my breath.

Without seeming to even move, she darted toward me with her lethal-looking, jagged fingernails out and ready to rip into my body. Before she could get too close, Ian flew in front of me and held up his hands as if to block her from reaching me. He turned his head to look back at me without dropping his arms and yelled something I couldn't hear, but I could easily read on his lips.

Run.

I didn't think twice.

I jumped up from the ground and ran back in the direction of the Manor, her furious screams echoing through the ruins and spurring me to run faster. Heedless of the rocks that blocked my way, I scraped my hands and knees as I vaulted over the stones, determined to put as much distance between the ghosts left at the ruins and me as I could.

It wasn't until I was past the stones and back on the path that I noticed the sky was much darker than it had been just a few minutes before. It was also much colder, and even though my body was heated from my frantic escape, I was still trembling from the cold as much as the surge of adrenaline coursing through after what had just happened.

I didn't slow down until I was nearly to the house, pausing to put my hands on my knees and breathing heavily. I looked back at the broken walls of the old castle and felt a different kind of dread. I had left Ian behind as he placed himself between the woman and me.

I think he had been denying being the one to attempt to drown me, and his actions today showed that he was protecting me rather than trying to hurt me. So if he wasn't the one that tried to hurt me, who was? And why had they? I was hardly important, only here to be the teacher of a sweet little girl.

Thoughts kept swirling as I continued walking, and the cuts and scrapes began to make themselves known. The air had noticeably warmed the further away I got from the evil that had saturated the ruins as soon as that woman had shown up. I thought of the story that Isla had told me, and I couldn't help but think there had to be more to it. There was a mystery surrounding this Manor and the family. Isla hadn't told me everything, and I was left wondering exactly what she had left out.

By the time I made it up to my room, I was shaking, contemplating if I should pack my bags and call Doogal to drive me back to the airport. I was willing to brave the anxiety of traveling just to get away from the terror of having a ghost attempting to kill me.

Starting the shower, I stripped off my dirty, torn clothes and stepped into the warm stream, hoping to wash off the events of earlier. With each movement and glance around me I prayed that I would be left alone to gather my thoughts and make a decision. This curse wasn't mine. It wasn't my fight. She had no right to terrorize me!

I let the tears fall as I scrubbed myself clean, watching the dirty water run down the drain. My heart was torn in two by the time I was done. I was scared, terrified of the woman. They called her a witch, and I believed they were right. No ordinary woman could possibly look or feel the way she did. Who else would be able to curse an entire family line?

But I also felt pulled to stay. The feeling was overwhelming, as if the Manor itself was begging me to stay. It felt like the Manor wanted me to help them, but I wasn't prepared for anything like this. I came here to teach, not to be haunted by ghosts.

I stepped out of the shower, wrapped a towel around my body, grabbing another one to dry my hair. I didn't want to abandon that sweet child. I didn't want to leave Isla after she had entrusted me with her daughter. The pain of my decision was breaking my heart.

I stepped into my bedroom, fully prepared to find my suitcase, and start packing it when I stopped short.

Ian Campbell was standing in the middle of my room with his back to me, facing one of the windows. His shoulders were hunched over as if he were upset by what had happened. If I had to guess, he would know that I was going to leave.

He turned around at my approach, and his green eyes flared as he took in my appearance. The feet that didn't quite touch the ground took a step in my direction before stopping, and he clenched his hands at his sides. But his eyes didn't lose any of their warmth.

His mouth moved, and as I tried to read his lips, I was shocked to realize I could hear faint sounds coming from him.

"Please... can't... Manor."

I shook my head, stuck between trying to understand what he was attempting to say and surprise that he was communicating verbally. "I don't understand." I turned away from him and threw open the wardrobe doors, searching for my suitcase without finding it. I turned around to survey the room, ignoring his form. My eyes landed on the bed, and I quickly walked over to it and knelt down to look under it.

In triumph, I dragged it out from under the bed frame and threw it on the bed, then startled. I froze to see his translucent hand covering mine, expecting to feel coldness come from him, but there was nothing but a very slight warmth.

I looked up at his face so close to mine and swallowed back my protest at the pleading look in his eyes.

"Lacey."

My eyes widened at his use of my name.

"Please." He stopped and squeezed his eyes briefly, his square jaw clenched tight at having to beg. *"Don't leave. I will protect you. The Manor, it... needs you."*

Six

For the rest of the day, I turned Ian's words over in my mind. I had stared into his mossy green eyes for several long moments until he faded away into nothingness. Once he had disappeared completely, I sat down heavily on the bed next to my suitcase and stared at it. I didn't get up until the alarm on my phone started ringing, startling me from my thoughts and letting me know that it was almost time for my next session with Olivia.

It was the little girl that calmed me enough to make a decision to stay. Ian Campbell had promised to protect me, and if the bathroom incident was anything to go by, he would do his best. I didn't know how he was able to stop the witch from hurting me, but he had proven that he was capable of it twice now.

I spent the night tossing and turning, and by the time the next morning rolled around, I had decided that I needed to solve the mystery as quickly as possible if I was going to stay here and if I ever wanted to get another full night of sleep again. I just had to figure out where to start. Isla had mentioned the library, and it seemed like the logical place to begin.

At breakfast, I approached the subject with her, trying to see if she would know anything that would point me in the right direction.

I stirred my coffee and thought of the best way to ask. "Isla," I paused, looking up as she gave me her attention. "The story you told me about your family's history. Are there books in the library about it? I'm... I guess I'm curious about it."

She cocked her head, studying me. "Well, I think there should be. I know my grandmother was adamant that no one speak about it. Once my grandfather died, it's possible she might have gotten rid of anything having to do with the curse."

She tapped her fingers on the wooden table, her eyes looking into mine, making me resist the need to squirm in my seat.

"Is there a reason?"

I shrugged and tried to keep my voice as even as possible. "It intrigues me." Which wasn't a lie. I didn't know how much to tell her. She didn't seem to be affected by what was going on around the Manor the way I was. Obviously, both she and Olivia knew about the voices, but I had a feeling that neither one had been tormented by them nightly, nor had they come face to face with the witch. I certainly didn't want to hurt her by letting her know that her recently deceased brother was hanging around and in contact with me.

"I guess I think that since I live here now, and I, you know, can hear the voices, I want to know why." I trailed off as she looked away from me and out the window.

"Others have tried to break the curse," she said, a sad tone in her voice. "After my da passed, my mam hired a few different people. They came in their strange clothes, with herbs they waved around. One would walk around ringing a bell and talking to the ghosts, telling them to leave. They all charged her a lot of money, promised that they had sent them to the light." She looked back at me. "It never worked."

She stood up and cleared our dishes, placing them in the sink for the staff that would come in after we left to tidy everything up. When she was done, she turned back to me and placed a hand that I couldn't help but notice had a slight tremble to it onto the table.

"Do you wonder why I hired you out of all the people that applied for the position, Lacey?"

I nodded my head. I had wondered about the answer to that question since the moment I received the email welcoming me to the position.

"It's funny about this place." She looked around the room and out the doorway that showed an elaborate hall that was in stark contrast to the simple, homey feel of the small kitchen. "It has always seemed to have a mind of its own. It has a way of making sure that decisions are made that it *wants* you to make. I don't know what books we may have left in our library here, but the last I heard, the library in the village will have what you are looking for. They have an entire section of local lore and history on the families, including ours." She gave me a tight smile and started to leave, but paused in the doorway just as I was about to rise from my seat, freezing my movements. "I'm sorry I pulled you into my family's curse, Lacey." She looked like she wanted to say something else, but she just nodded her head and left.

I waited until the clicking of her heels faded before I stood up from my chair, scooting it back under the table. I nervously wiped my hands on the soft material of the dress I had decided to wear today and began to walk down the long hallway toward the large doors that hid the library from view. I could feel my anxiety creeping up the closer I got for the first time since I had arrived.

I rubbed at my wrist, feeling the bones under my skin, trying to concentrate on that one thing. When it didn't seem to help, I stood in front of the doors and tapped my hand, my wrist, and my fingers.

"Hand." I tapped. "Wrist." Tap. "Fingers." Tap.

What was I going to find? Would it be anything useful? Would I find anything at all?

Hand. Wrist. Fingers.

Tap. Tap. Tap.

Finally, I took a deep breath and swung the door open. Inside was the smell one would expect from a room full of old books–dust, slightly decaying paper, with a hint of amber and vanilla. It was there, along with the scent of lemons from the polish someone had used on the wood recently. I stood there, just taking in the sight of the tall shelves that had to be ten feet in height. It was dark, with heavy drapes pulled tight against the large windows to keep the harmful sunlight from damaging the older tomes that were nestled on the shelves. It was beautiful.

I walked over toward the nearest standing lamp and twisted the knob to raise the brightness high enough to see properly and to chase away some of the gloom. I walked to another one a few feet away and did the same before just standing there, looking around the spacious room.

I had no idea where to start. Somewhere inside this room could be the key to ending the curse, or there could be nothing at all. But I had to start somewhere. I walked to the nearest shelf and walked along it, lightly trailing my finger over the edge of the wood as I read the spines. The shelf contained several classics from the last century, many that I had read in school or read for my own pleasure.

I walked to the next shelf and did the same. And the next. And the next. There were many bestsellers and many books someone would expect from a lover of books from the last few decades. I found a section full of Shakespeare, Poe, Faulkner, and then Rice and King.

What I didn't find were any books about family curses.

I stood in the middle of the room with my hands on my hips and glared. I turned in a circle, trying to see if I had missed any shelves, maybe missing one, as I had moved throughout the room. It was pretty freaking large, after all.

Movement out of the corner of my eye caught my attention, and I turned to see a maid wearing a black dress walk in with an old-fashioned feather duster. I had to blink twice when I realized that she wasn't solid. I could see straight through her to the shelves on the other side of the room.

I couldn't take my eyes off of the apparition as she stopped to dust a table with a brass statue on it and then the shelf next to her. It wasn't until she had dusted for several minutes and my breaths were coming in small pants that she turned to me and curtsied.

I could do nothing but continue to stare at her, not knowing how I should react to who was obviously a ghost of a maid that used to work in the Manor ages ago.

"Save us, Miss."

I stumbled back as her lips moved, but the sound seemed to come from everywhere around the room.

She pointed to a shelf high up in the corner of the room that would need the rolling ladder to reach, then turned around to walk back the way she had come, fading before my eyes.

I swallowed hard and walked on trembling legs over to the wall and placed a shaky hand on the ladder to drag it over to the corner. I took a deep breath and then placed one foot on the ladder, testing its durability before climbing up to the top of the shelf.

It was dark in the corner, and the light didn't reach this far into the room, so I took my phone out of the pocket of my dress and turned on the flashlight. The books that were on the shelf were not traditionally published books. They looked like journals. I set my phone down on the shelf, light up, and carefully slid the first one out. I opened it up as gently as I could. It had a leather cover, and the pages were hand sewn to the binding. It was beautiful work.

The inside of the first page had a name written, and I had to lean closer to the light to read it.

Colleen Campbell 1836

MY BREATH CAUGHT as I realized this was the second Lady of the Manor. What had she known about what happened to her mother-in-law? I looked back at the line of journals that all looked the same. There were five in total. I carefully went to the last page of the journal I held in my hand to check the date. 1838.

This journal covered two years' time. If they each had two years of writing in them, that would give me ten years of history to learn. Would it be enough?

The alarm on my phone started ringing next to me on the shelf, startling me so badly that I jumped, causing my foot to slip off the rung. I had to drop the book to try to stop myself from falling. I yelped and grabbed onto the shelf with both hands, but I had no real grip on the smooth surface, with my weight trying to pull me backward.

I heard the book thump as it hit the ground and knew I was about to be next when I felt a strong grip wrap around my waist.

"Easy, lass. You're safe."

I was able to set my foot firmly back onto the rung and grip the sides of the ladder with my shaking hands. I turned to look at Ian, knowing I had him to thank for saving me... again. It was a bit startling to see him hovering in the air several feet above the ground as I stood there clinging to the ladder.

I let out a puff of breath as my heart tried to settle itself back into a normal rate. "Thank you," I whispered, noticing how close our faces were. Had he been as solid yesterday as he appeared now?

His eyes looked down at my lips as I said the words, then looked back up at my face before carefully letting go of my waist and nodding once in acknowledgment. He drifted back as he watched me take another deep breath and turn to reach up and grab my phone, dropping it carefully in my pocket before climbing down from the ladder.

By the time I reached the floor, he was there beside me, holding the journal I had dropped in my haste. It was strange how solid yet incorporeal he looked at the same time. I could see the leather through his fingers, but he had a firm grip on the book.

I reached out, and he placed it in my hand, careful not to touch me. I was almost disappointed and felt a small pang of hurt that he was suddenly avoiding me.

"You must be more careful, Lacey Conrad. I can't be everywhere all the time."

My back straightened at his words, and I couldn't stop myself from snapping out at him. "I didn't ask you for your help, Ian Campbell."

"Even so, it appears as if I am needed *anyway."* I didn't miss the way he said *needed*, as though it implied something more. He bowed his head in a formal manner and backed away as his form faded.

If he hadn't disappeared completely, I would have been tempted to throw the journal at his ridiculously handsome head. I growled under my breath at his audacity and then turned the leather-bound book over in my hand, inspecting it for any damage from the fall. There was some bending at the top corner that hadn't been there before, but overall it seemed to be unscathed. I breathed out in relief and then hurried to the door when I heard Oliva's crutches tapping on the marble hallway.

I closed the doors behind me and waved to her with a smile as I met her at the door to the kitchen.

"Hello, sweetheart. Are you ready to go over some shapes today?"

As she greeted me and announced her eagerness to get started, I thanked Chasity and then helped Olivia get settled into her seat at the table with her school supplies that were neatly kept in a box on a shelf near the window.

We settled in to learn, but my mind never strayed far from the small book I'd slipped onto the chair beside me, out of sight.

Seven

I decided that the library was as good a place as any to start reading the journal, so I set up a reading nook in a comfortable chair, a throw, and a warm cup of tea. Once I was settled in, I wiped my hands on the blanket nervously before finally reaching for the leather-bound book.

Opening it carefully, doing my best not to crack the binding or tear the fragile pages. I passed the first page that had the name Colleen Campbell written in a fancy script that I would never be able to duplicate and flipped to the first entry. It only took a minute to get lost in her words.

March 13th

Tomorrow is my wedding day!

All my sisters are so jealous of my good fortune in landing the best match in the entire area. Conal Campbell is the most handsome man I have ever seen, and tomorrow he becomes my husband. I could just die!

SHE WAS SO excited to get married. I could just picture this young woman huddled in her bed, writing instead of being able to sleep. I continued reading about her dress and the flowers that would be dressing the chapel. I wondered if she knew what waited for her at the Manor.

> March 15th
> Last night was so much more than I could ever have imagined.
> Our wedding was absolutely perfect. The whole town turned up to witness our vows. I felt like a princess.
> But last night...
> I knew about relations between a man and woman. My mam had done her best to prepare me, but she could never have prepared me for THAT.

I COULDN'T HELP my grin. Conal had obviously rocked her world, and good for her. Well done, Conal.

> March 18th
> That woman is a monster.
> I don't think Conal believes me when I tell him that his mother gives me evil looks. She is so... sinister. Everyone has heard the story of what happened to her husband. I'm sure the only reason she hasn't been locked away

somewhere is because of her status. She shouldn't be here terrorizing the staff.

April 10th

I'm pregnant. Oh my lord, I just admitted it. I haven't told Conal yet, but I just know he's going to be thrilled.

Mrs. Campbell has been eying me even more lately. I think she suspects I am with child, and that scares me.

April 22nd

My cat was found this morning. Oh, I can barely breathe. My poor, lovely Imogen. I don't believe she was destroyed by wild dogs like they are telling me. No dog could have slit her throat so neatly. I just know it was that woman.

I PICKED up my cold cup, needing to take a break from the scenes that were unfolding in the journal. Colleen knew that her mother-in-law was evil. Why hadn't anyone done something to stop her? What a horrible thing to go through.

June 20th

I told Conal today that I was going to leave him.

That woman has always been touched, but now she will scream the most awful scream, day and night. I just can't stay here under the same roof with her any longer.

My favorite dress was shredded, completely in tatters. I found it lying under our bed. Why would she do that? I am frightened for the life of my unborn child. I can see in her eyes that she wants to hurt me next.

June 22nd
Conal begged me to stay.
He told me how much he loved me and promised to keep his mother away from me. I want to believe him; I do. And, oh, how I love him, too. But I am still so scared. Even right now, I can hear her screaming in her wing where he demanded she stay. She's been raising such a ruckus, breaking things and smashing dishes.

FOR THE NEXT SEVERAL MONTHS, Colleen focused only on her child and went into great detail about what she was doing to prepare the nursery. Her words sent a pang through me at the pure love she already had for her child. It was beautiful. Other than the witch, her life sounded nearly perfect, with a doting husband and a new kitten she'd named Walter. It wasn't until after the birth of her healthy baby boy that things became much worse, and I finally learned the name of the woman that caused the devastation in the family for the last 190 or so years.

> *January 10th*
>
> *She got out of her wing somehow. I woke up to see Elspeth Campbell standing over my Edwin's cradle. Her eyes were wild as she looked down at my little baby, and all I could do was scream and scream and scream. Conal forced her back into her rooms, but I can't say how shaken up the episode made me.*
>
> *There are rumors in the house that she has been chanting a lot and drawing on the walls with the soot from her fireplace. The whispers are growing louder.*
>
> *Elspeth Campbell is a witch.*

THE REST OF THE YEAR, the entries only focused on the baby as he did all the things that babies did. Her love for him was precious to read; she described every tooth, every smile, his first crawl and somewhere in his babbling, she was certain he was saying mama. As I closed the book on the last entry a full two years after her announcement of getting married, it felt like I had gotten to know Colleen on an intimate level. She was just a young woman that became a young mother, worried about her child.

During that first year of the baby's life, there were no more incidents with Elspeth, and I think I was just as relieved as Colleen must have been. I looked over toward the shelf where the other four journals sat, waiting for me to read. It would have to wait until the morning. It was already late, and I knew if I started reading, I wouldn't be able to make myself stop.

I stood up and stretched my back, carefully placing the journal on the side table, knowing it would be fine until tomorrow when I would replace it in its rightful spot. I just couldn't make myself climb that ladder again this late at night. I set the throw in the chair and left the teacup for tomorrow, too. Everything could wait. I needed to get to bed.

As I started walking out of the library, the hairs on the back of my neck stood up on end, and I rubbed my hands over my arms, picking up my pace. My footsteps echoed around the great hall as I crossed the open space. I started jogging up the stairs as the whispers began. And then more joined. And then more. Until it felt like every ancestor, staff member, or anyone who had ever lived here was speaking all at once.

There were so many of them I couldn't discern any specific words. I wanted to cover my ears to block them out, but I knew it wouldn't help. It wasn't until I was at the top of the stairs that the first ghost materialized just a few feet away.

Stop the witch!

I swallowed hard and walked past quickly, trying to ignore the young woman dressed as a servant. When I turned the corner to head down the long hall to my bedroom, a man in a hat and coat appeared.

Ye must help us.

"Please stop," I whispered back, my heart pounding as I started running down the hall. I wasn't almost to my room when the third one appeared at the end of the hall.

Release us!

"I don't know how!" I yelled as I fumbled with the door and swung it open, darting for safety inside. I slammed it closed behind me and leaned my back against the door, my hands pressed flat against it as my whole body trembled. I squeezed my eyes closed and tapped the door with my fingertips.

I got my bearing and finally stumbled forward on shaky knees and dove for the bed, not even trying to take off any of my clothing. I kicked off my shoes and slid between the sheets, only then realizing I had left the lights on. I couldn't be bothered with them. They could stay on all night for all I cared. I wasn't leaving the bed until the sun was back in the sky.

As I lay there trying to calm down, I felt a hand glide over my shoulder through the thick blanket covering me. I jolted and tried to scramble back, a scream lodged in my throat.

"Shh, darling. You are safe."

I froze and blinked up at Ian as he sat on the edge of my bed.

"Wh-what are you doing here?" I whispered through my clogged throat.

"I told you I would keep you safe. I will stay until you fall asleep."

"Why are they doing this to me? I'm not a part of your family."

He frowned and removed his hand from my shoulder, clenching them in his lap. *"I do not know. Somehow, the Manor knows you are important."*

I shook my head. I didn't want to be important to the stupid Manor. No one asked me if I wanted to be involved in all this. I watched him as he watched me. I couldn't help but notice again how handsome he was. I swallowed. How handsome he *used to be*. Ian was a ghost, just like the others.

His eyes dropped to my lips as they had done before, then raised back up to my eyes. He stood up from the bed, and I almost reached out to grab him to pull him back beside me. For some reason, he made me feel safe. He seemed to know what I was thinking because he murmured to me as he walked over to the chair in the corner.

"I will watch over you, Lacey Conrad. You can sleep peacefully."

I just blinked as his translucent body settled into the chair and crossed a leg over one knee. As I stared at him, I felt my eyes grow heavy. The next thing I knew, my alarm was ringing in my pocket, and Ian Campbell was gone.

Eight

"Good morning, Lacey." Isla held out a cup toward me without me even having to ask, and I gave her a grateful smile as I took it in both of my hands. I simply stood there a moment and breathed in the rich aroma of the coffee, enjoying the warmth of the mug in my hands. "I realized that I haven't shown you the conservatory yet."

I looked up from stirring a bit of sugar into my cup and smiled. "I have to admit, I've been really curious. Seeing it from the outside as I passed was already an experience. I can't wait to see the inside."

"There's a reason why it's my favorite room in the whole house." She smiled and then looked at her phone to check the time. "I have about fifteen minutes before I have to run out of the door."

We began walking the short distance to the glass encased room just beyond the great hall. From the outside, it had looked huge, and I had a feeling that the inside was going to be massive. I was beginning to understand that nothing about this house had been done in moderation.

As we approached the door, I saw all the thick, leafy green plants filling the space along the glass wall, but not much beyond that. Isla's serious tone pulled me from my eagerness to finally see what was beyond.

"The conservatory was added on to the structure of the house close to fifty years ago." She seemed to hesitate for a minute before finally just saying whatever she was holding back. "So far, there have been no reports of the witch by anyone while inside." She shrugged. "Of course, that could be because very few people go inside. I have a couple of dedicated house staff members that tend to the plants and the hot tub, but other than myself and Olivia, no one else enters."

She opened the door and allowed me to enter first. Immediately, I felt a blast of warm, humid air cover me. The scent of earth and floral fragrance permeated the air, and I couldn't have stopped myself from breathing even deeper if I'd tried.

Taking a few steps forward, I took in the, indeed, massive room. There was a workbench near an outdoor glass wall, the area looked like it was set up specifically for a younger child to explore the art of gardening and enjoy getting dirt on their hands. The thought of Olivia in here, enjoying playing in the dirt, and gardening made me smile fondly.

I could hear water trickling somewhere nearby, but had yet to actually catch sight of it. What I did see was a small jacuzzi type of pool, complete with wisps of steam wafting from the top, adding to the heat and humidity of the cavernous room. I turned back to Isla with a grin, practically making my face ache with how big it was, but immediately dropped it when I saw her still standing there by the door, wringing her hands.

"Isla?" I hesitantly asked, frozen to the spot. An icy tremor of dread ran over my spine at the sudden fear that she was about to fire me. Why was it just a day ago I wanted to escape from here, wanting to run far from the ghosts, the witch, Ian...

But now, standing here in front of Isla, who held my immediate future in her hands, I was ready to drop to my knees on the tile floor and beg for her to let me stay. I couldn't think about all the reasons why at the moment. It was something I would have to examine later when I had a moment to myself. When I could be honest.

Her smile was weak, and she looked a bit... ashamed? I tilted my head as I studied her, my confusion growing.

"I honestly had no idea that this place was going to affect you this way, Lacey. I feel terrible that I hadn't at least warned you of the possibilities before inviting you here to take the job with my daughter." She sighed and walked over toward an fragrant tree that was practically dripping in oranges. "I know we talked about it already, but the guilt has been eating me alive."

She reached out and firmly gripped a ripe orange, giving it a sharp twist and pull. She held up the orange and gave a small grin. "Lunch." Her expression faded almost instantly when she looked back at me.

I shook my head. "You couldn't have known." She didn't even know everything that had been happening. I hadn't told her about being physically attacked. As far as Isla was aware, I had only heard whispers and seen a few ghosts. If she knew the whole truth, she'd likely fire me just to get me away from here.

"No, but as a prospective employer, I should have provided you with full disclosure." She turned to me, giving me her full attention, and folded her hands behind her back. She looked very serious at that moment, and I could picture her as a teacher in front of her classroom or a boss giving instructions to her employees. I guess that second one was pretty spot-on. "I have thought about it quite a bit and have come to the conclusion that there are only two options here that satisfy both of us."

I gripped my coffee cup firmly in both hands to steady the shakiness that I wanted to hide. I gave her a nod to let her know I was listening, but I couldn't speak, not until I knew if she was firing me or if I would be able to stay and try to help this family end the curse once and for all.

"Right. Well, one, you can leave, and I will provide you with a settlement of the equivalent of one year's pay, room, and board. Exactly what your services would have been worth had you been able to stay." My jaw had dropped somewhere midway through her words.

"That's... that's too much, Isla!"

"Perhaps, but it is my fault that you are having trouble sleeping." Her eyes studied my face as they ran over the features that I knew were drawn and tired-looking. "Honestly, I have never seen anyone as affected by the Manor and the ghosts as you are. While it pains me to see you this way, it does intrigue me as to why. But your well-being should always come first. So, your first choice is to leave."

I didn't fail to notice that she did not call it being fired. She obviously wanted to make sure it was clear that whatever my decision was, it came only from me. "And the second option?"

She looked around the conservatory. "This has always been my most favorite place on earth. I have never felt safer or happier than when I am in here, either working on the plants or just soaking in the hot tub. I was hoping that you could take some time to enjoy it. Maybe get some rest. I know it's a bit humid and warm, but it's very peaceful." She looked around again, and her shoulders dropped as she looked back at me. "I've never heard nor seen anything in here. I can't promise that it is safe from ghosts. But, if it helps you at all, please, take advantage of the place."

"Isla, this is your sanctuary. I couldn't possibly..." She held up her hand, cutting off my words before looking at her phone and grimacing.

"I'm so sorry. I really do have to get going. But I wanted to give you these two options. They were the only ones that I was able to come up with that would benefit you the most. Please, feel free to spend time in here today to relax and think on it. You can let me know your decision tonight when I get home, okay?"

I nodded as she gave me a warm smile, obviously feeling better since she had given me her options. I understood guilt better than most people and knew what it could do to a person, even if it wasn't their fault. I had felt plenty of it over the years as I grew up, knowing that I was making my parent's lives harder. I had also spent quite a bit of time in therapy to help manage my anxiety disorder, and part of that was learning to accept that it wasn't my fault that I was wired a little differently.

"Okay, great!" She turned to the door and gripped the handle, but paused before walking out the door. "We really are glad you came here, Lacey. I just wanted you to know that. Olivia loves you. I know it's been such a short time, but I know we would both be sad to lose you already. I don't want to pressure you, but I wanted you to know that. Okay?"

She gave me one last smile and walked out the door when I gave her another short, jerky nod. As soon as she was gone, I looked up at the glass ceiling high above and blinked rapidly. Everything about this place had been different from what I had expected to experience. I had been on a rollercoaster of emotions since arriving. I was well on my way to making a good friend in Isla, and Olivia was the easiest little sweetheart to fall in love with. Then there was a green eyed ghost that I was becoming more and more intrigued by as the days passed. I didn't have to think about it. There was no question of where my path lay after today. I was staying. And as long as I was here, I would do everything I could to help this family.

"She doesn't really open up to people very often, you know."

I whirled around at the sound of Ian's voice, which was getting stronger each day. He was also getting more... condensed? Thicker? Solid? What did ghosts become as they became less incorporeal? I watched as he reached out for an orange and tried to grip it in his hand, but all that happened is it wavered just a little, as if it had been blown by a gentle breeze.

My eyes widened, and I looked back at Ian in shock that he had even managed to do that much, but his jaw was clenched hard as he glared at the orange. He turned to look at me and took the couple of steps needed to bring us closer together. His nearly but not quite solid form was the same as always. It hadn't changed since the first time I saw him. He was dressed casually, wearing a long-sleeve shirt and dark jeans. He looked like he was relaxing at home for the day. My heart ached when I realized that was exactly what he *had* been doing before he died. Before the witch killed him by pushing him off of his balcony, the same as she had done her own husband nearly two hundred years ago.

He raised his hand as he looked down at me, his green eyes tracing over the features of my face. His finger moved as if it were tracing every path that he had taken with his eyes. *"You won't do anything to hurt my sister, will you, darling?"*

I shook my head and swallowed at the faint threat I heard in his voice even as the endearment ran through me like a warm river, filling me up with heat. He studied me for a long minute, just continuing to move his finger in a back-and-forth motion that could only have been his way of tracing my bottom lip.

Looking up at him, something seemed to fill his eyes, giving them a bit of warmth. The anger that had been there since I first saw him disappearing as he looked back at me. I couldn't stop myself from letting out a shaky breath and running my tongue over the lip that I wished I could feel his touch.

His pupils dilated as they watched my tongue swipe across where his fingers were. They darted to mine, and I could have sworn he let out a rumble from his chest. He ran his ghostly thumb over my lip once more before stepping back, and his eyes grew cold once again.

"I will be seeing you again soon. Keep my niece safe, yes?"

I nodded numbly as he disappeared, and once he was gone, I shakily lifted a hand to my mouth. Because I could have sworn that last brush of his thumb... I felt it.

Nine

I smiled down at the tiny curly-haired head of Olivia as she attempted to trace over the shapes that I had drawn for her. She was like a sponge, soaking up all the knowledge I gave her. We only had to go over the same thing a couple of times before she was ready to move on. I was willing to go at her pace, with a little backtracking to make sure that she didn't forget what I had already gone over with her.

"Miss Olivia," Chastity called out gently from the doorway, gaining both of our attention. The more I saw her, the more I realized that I judged Chastity a little too quickly the first night I met her. She was quiet and reserved toward the rest of us, but patient and kind to Olivia, and that was all that mattered. I sensed that she was just the kind of person who didn't relax easily with strangers. I could completely understand that.

I looked back at Olivia and grinned as she popped her head up, her little tongue sticking out of the corner of her mouth from the intense concentration. "Go on, sweetie. I'll get this put away. I will see you later, okay?" I couldn't resist running my hand lightly over her red curls.

She nodded enthusiastically and carefully slid her arms into the grips of her crutches. Chastity came forward, ready to help if needed, but allowing Olivia to try on her own. It was easy to want to jump forward and do things for the little girl, but I understood the need for her independence. She was going to face a lifetime of people trying to take advantage of her or thinking less of her for her disability. Those of us that are closest to her have the opportunity to show her while she's young that she is just as capable as anyone else.

I started gathering our papers together and was tapping the stack on the table when Olivia startled me by giving me a quick hug before dashing out of the room, her little crutches making tapping sounds echo through the great hall. "Bye, sweetheart!" I called out with a chuckle and blinked back the wetness in my eyes at her gesture. Olivia had been free with her hugs since the day we met, but for some reason, I had been feeling more emotional since I woke up this morning.

I thought back to the night before and the way Ian had hovered over me, his concern written on his face. He was confusing me. One minute he seemed cold, and I worried that he was upset at my presence in his family home. Then other times, when his eyes ran over my face or lingered on my lips the way they had that morning in the conservatory...

I shook my head and tried to dismiss the thoughts that had been invading my mind throughout the day. My morning had been spent in the library reading through the four remaining journals of Colleen Campbell's. I had been surprised to find them neatly stacked on the table next to the chair I had claimed as my own for reading, and since no one else, well, no one that wasn't a ghost, knew what I had been up to, I could only surmise that Ian had set them out for me.

After a few more entries, I ended up mostly scanning through the passages as the small family lived their lives in mid-nineteenth-century Scotland. There was heartbreak as Colleen discovered her body couldn't seem to carry a second baby to term. There was joy and pride as her son grew and achieved high marks in his schooling. There was also a deep, emotional connection between Colleen and the Lord of the Manor; it was clear they were very much in love. So when her husband died in a sudden and unexplainable way nearly ten years after the beginning of their relationship, she was understandably distraught.

I'd had to close the journal soon after that entry in order to meet Oliva for her next teaching session and I spent the following hour doing everything I could to place all my attention on her. But now that my time was my own again, I was desperate to get back to the library. There were very few entries left in the journal I was reading and I was desperate to get back to learning more about the Manor and its occupants. I also couldn't help but wonder if I'd see Ian there again.

My steps were hurried and echoed throughout the great hall as I rushed toward the library. When I entered, I went straight to the area I had claimed as my reading nook, but stopped short and stared at the empty space where the journals had last been. Even the throw I had been using to ward off the chill of the large space was gone.

I spun in a circle, confusion running through me as I took in the area. It was as if I had never been in there at all. I stalked over towards the shelf in the far corner, wondering if perhaps a well-meaning member of the cleaning staff had put the books away. I didn't even have to climb the ladder to realize they were all gone, including the first one in the series of journals.

Dread washed over me and I couldn't believe what I was seeing. Where had everything gone? I thought of who might have removed them and why, but it didn't make sense. Isla had told me I could look through the library. I couldn't see her instructing someone to get rid of the only chance I had of learning about the history of the Manor or the witch that seemed hell-bent on destroying her own legacy.

I hung my head in defeat as I tried to think of what other options I had. There was a library in the village. Perhaps there would be something there. I was out of ideas, so I pulled my phone from my pocket to look at the time. It was just past three in the afternoon. The library had to be still open for at least another hour.

I hurried out of the library and jogged up the stairs toward my room to grab a jacket to ward off the chilly autumn air and was back to crossing the expanse of the great hall within a few short minutes. I pulled my phone back out of my pocket to give Doogal a call for a ride.

"Uh, hi, Doogal," I said awkwardly, as I opened the heavy front door. "This is Lacey. You said I could call you for a ride?"

"Of course, Miss. Would ye be wanting a ride to the village, then?"

I breathed out a relieved breath. "Yes, sir. Do you mind? If you have time, that is…"

"Of course, 'tis no trouble at all. You just sit tight, and I will bring the car around in just a minute, Miss."

"Thank you so much!"

I hit end call and slipped the phone back into the pocket of my slacks, and smoothed my blouse down under my jacket in nervousness. I hadn't left the house since the day I went to the ruins. It seemed like weeks ago, but I realized it had only been days. So much had happened in such a short amount of time. I could hardly believe it when I thought back to the day I entered the Manor for the first time.

I was going to visit the village and would have to talk to strangers. While I was eager to see what I could learn from the local library, I wasn't looking forward to being out in public again. If I could get away with never leaving the house, I probably would.

Doogal's arrival interrupted my musings, and every step I took toward the waiting car had my anxiety rising higher. I slipped into the seat and quickly pulled the belt across my lap, giving Doogal a shaky smile.

"Thank you again for this. I'm sorry if I interrupted you."

He waved a weathered hand as if wiping my apology away. "Nonsense. There's nothing that can't wait for a nice trip to the village." He guided the car around the large circular drive, and we passed the giant water fountain that was bubbling away between the two roads. "So where is it we are headed?"

"I'd like to take a look at the library, if you think it's open at this time?"

His chuckle was rusty sounding. "Oh, aye. If there is one building that is always open, it's the library."

That sounded like it had an interesting story behind it, but he didn't elaborate. The ride was quick, and before I had a chance to get a good look around the small town, we were slowing to a stop in front of a building with large windows and several barrels along the front filled with colorful flowers. I was immediately enamored with the charming look of the building.

It was inviting, and when I stepped through the door, I saw large, overstuffed leather chairs arranged throughout the large space. Each was arranged next to the tall wooden shelves filled with colorful book covers.

My fingers itched to drift over the shelves until I found something that I could sink into. It would be something full of passion and mystery. And absolutely no ghosts.

Instead of giving in to the urge, I made my way to the large circular desk in the center of the room. A woman with a kind smile, glasses perched on her nose, and a gray bun on the top of her head smiled broadly at me.

"Why, hello there, stranger! What can I do for you here in our lovely village library?"

I couldn't help but relax at her welcoming smile. "Hi, the place is wonderful." I tucked a strand of hair that escaped from my ponytail behind my ear. "I just moved into Moreland Manor, and since I am a teacher, I couldn't help my curiosity about the history of the place. Do you have any books about the local lore?" I didn't miss the way her smile dimmed a little, and a strange look flitted across her face too quickly for me to decipher the meaning.

"Oh, dear. Well, we do have a few books, but they weren't written by locals. You won't find much beyond the local flora and fauna. And a tale or two about when the castle was still standing. Unfortunately, there was a fire back in the early twenties." She grinned. "The 1920s, that would be. The village lost all kinds of records that were priceless to us. What kind of information are you looking for, in particular?"

My cheeks heated up, and I tapped my fingertips on the varnished wooden desktop. "Umm, well. I talked with Isla the other day, and she was talking about her ancestors. And..." I rolled my lips together before just blurting it out. "I wanted to see if you had any information about the original Lady of the Manor, Elspeth Campbell."

She immediately darted her eyes around the room and then lowered her voice. "Are ye sure, Miss? That's a name that people of this village don't like to talk about much."

I thought about the missing journals, the ghosts that seemed determined to haunt me until I released them from their unending torture, and about Ian. The last one had me pausing before biting my lip and then giving a quick nod. "Yes, ma'am. I don't know how to explain it. I just..." I blew out a breath. "I need to know how to help them." I finished with a whisper.

"Oh, dear." She looked around one more time before catching the eye of a young woman that was a perfect younger version of the one in front of me. "Meagan, take over the desk for a little while, will you, love? I'm going to take our ghost hunter here to see your great gran."

Meagan looked surprised and intrigued. "Oh? That's interesting."

"It is. And I'll tell you all about it later." She reached under the counter and pulled out a thin cardigan before shrugging it on. "I won't be long."

The young woman nodded as she headed around to the inside of the circular desk. "Not a problem. Go on now. Gran will be ready for a nap soon. Best catch her before she gets so tired that she nods off instead of chats."

The older librarian started toward the front door and jerked her head for me to follow. I scrambled over towards her, a bit overwhelmed as to what was happening so quickly. "Are you sure she'll want to talk to me? I don't want to intrude."

"Oh, my gran loves to talk to everyone. Never met a word she didn't like. But truthfully, she is probably the best person to talk to in all of Scotland." She gave me a conspiratorial grin and then pushed through the door and started walking down the cobblestone walkway. "You see, she used to work at the Manor when she was a young woman. The things my gran used to tell me when I was a wee lass." She shook her head. "I was fascinated by the stories. Though truth be told, I often had a few nights of lost sleep over those stories as well. I'm Moira. What's your name, love?"

"I'm sorry, how rude of me. My name is Lacey Conrad. Isla Campbell hired me to teach Olivia."

Moira's tone was warm as she spoke. "Of course she did. That lovely woman would do anything for her wee daughter. That is the sweetest child. It's a shame what her father did to them both. A downright shame, I tell ya! What man could walk out on their newborn child and wife straight out of labor that way? Not a man at all! He's a right numpty he is, and good riddance to 'em! Those sweet girls are much better off without." She sniffed and nodded her head decisively as my heart silently broke for Olivia and Isla.

I had known it was something awful, but to find out he had left them while they were still in the hospital tore my heart in two. I discreetly wiped my eyes as we came to a stop in front of a small, but tidy cottage that had the same type of flowers from outside the library overflowing the gardens in the front yard.

"Oh, dear, none of that now. Yes, those girls have had a hard run of it, losing their man and then losing their brother and uncle just recently. But those girls are stronger than anyone knows. They will only get stronger. That little girl will go on to do great things, mark my words." She twisted the knob and held the door open for me to enter first. "Now, let's get you settled with a nice cup of tea, shall we? You're going to need refreshments for the story my gran is about to tell you. Just try not to let her get too worked up, okay?"

Ten

The inside was as lovely as the outside, and I waited until Moira led me into a small sitting room with a settee and two armchairs. In one of the chairs sat an elderly woman dozing by a low burning fire. She looked to be in her late eighties, perhaps, and the lines on her face told of the many adventures and tales she'd lived.

Moira walked over to the woman and gave me a wink before gently tapping the back of the woman's hand. "Gran, I brought you a visitor."

I glanced around awkwardly, wringing my hands in front of me. I wanted to tell Moira that I would come back at a different time, one when this obviously very elderly and frail woman wasn't sleeping soundly while looking so cozy in an afghan blanket. I was feeling like a monster when she blinked her eyes open and focused on Moira.

"Well, what yer doin', girl? Get yer gran some tea."

My grin was hard to hide when she turned to look up at me.

"Hello, I'm Lacey." I spoke softly, resisting the urge to curtsy.

She nodded and patted the arm of the chair next to hers. "I know who ye are, child. Been expecting you. Now sit down before ye give me a crick in my neck."

Shocked, I darted my eyes over to meet Moira's. She looked taken aback by this, but she didn't look scared. I, however, was sure my unease was in every stiff line of my body. Nevertheless, I took the seat she wanted me to sit in and did my best to relax, though I knew it was impossible.

"Alright, I'll be right back with your tea, gran." Moira said, as she eyed the two of us before backing out of the room.

"I don't understand," I whispered softly.

"No one understands," she said as she straightened her blanket. "Ye might as well settle in and relax a little. 'Tis a story I need to tell ye."

"Is it about the Manor?"

"Aye, the Manor, the witch, the ghosts. Ye know all about that, don't ye, girl?" She eyed me knowingly, and I felt like a bug pinned under her gaze. Somehow, she knew everything about me without me having to say a word. All I could do was nod in disbelief. "Right," she sighed. "'Tis far past time to end things. I think the Manor has been waiting for a very long time for ye to arrive."

I shook my head. "I'm sorry, I really don't understand what any of this means. But, I am willing to do what I need to in order to free all those people trapped in the Manor. They scare me, I'm not going to lie, but what I've been able to learn about Elspeth already, she was awful when alive. Now that she's dead... I worry about what she is truly capable of. I worry that Isla and Olivia may be in danger, too."

"Dear girl, the one ye should be most concerned about is *ye*."

Moira chose that moment to bustle back into the room, carrying a tray with teacups and sugar. She smiled a big, overly cheerful smile. She was clearly not a fan of how this meeting was proceeding. I had to admit; I was a bit creeped out by it myself. "Here we are, loves. Steaming tea and a warm fire." She served us both tea in delicate cups and settled onto the small sofa with a cup of her own after placing another log gently onto the simmering fire.

Her gran began speaking again after taking a delicate sip of her tea, the cup rattling just a bit as she set it down on the saucer sitting on the small table between our chairs. Her voice was raspy with age, but rang out clearly in her gentle Scottish brogue. "I was a young lass of seventeen when I began working at the Manor. It was a coveted position here in the village. Many wanted to work there as they paid well and treated the help fairly.

"We had all heard the stories of the ghosts that haunted the Manor, and most of us had grown up with the stories of the witch. Our parents would sometimes use the tales as a way to keep us in line. 'Stay in bed or the witch will get ye'." She chuckled softly while staring at the fire as if playing back long forgotten memories in her mind. Then her chuckle abruptly cut off, and her tone became more serious.

"They were true," she confessed. "Every rumor and story. I worked there for years alongside my gran, who was the head housekeeper. She always bade me go home before nightfall. I just thought she didn't want me to walk in the dark. Instead, she was trying to keep me safe." She brought the cup back to her lips, and I couldn't help but notice that her gnarled hands were shaking much more than when she had started her story, and her eyes were glassy with unshed tears.

"My gran had been seeing the ghosts for a while, but kept that information to herself, trying to protect me, I suppose. Or maybe she thought she would lose her position. It wasn't until she had come home white as a sheet and shaken to her core one night that she sat me down and told me that she didn't want me working there anymore. Of course, I protested. It was excellent money for a girl my age. I was saving up for beautiful clothing and jewelry, thinking it might attract me a beau. But when I continued to resist, she finally told me of her experience.

"That night, she had seen the witch. She told me how she first heard the screams—as if someone were walking along the corridors shrieking in rage. When she left the room she had been tidying, the witch caught sight of my gran and flew straight at her. Gran said it felt like icy claws had raked over her face. She truly believed the witch had torn her flesh to ribbons. It wasn't until she ran to a mirror that she saw her skin was intact and had no marks. All except for one. She showed me the long scratch on her neck that had bled enough to soak into her shirt."

"I quit working as she had asked. But she didn't." She paused for a long moment as she stared into the fire with a haunted look on her face. I could see the story was affecting her in a way that made her already aged face look gaunt and drawn. "She continued to work there since it was good pay and she had mouths to feed. A week later, she didn't come home."

Her watery blue eyes turned towards me then, and I sucked in a breath. I had been hanging on her every word, but at that moment, I wasn't sure I wanted her to continue. I wanted nothing more than to jump up and leave the cozy cottage. Whatever had happened to her gran was enough to have changed her life in a horrible way.

"They found her body in a spare room. Her eyes were wide open, frozen in fear. There were no injuries on her except for that one scratch that had been almost healed from days before. No one could tell me what killed her or if she had died from a heart attack. I had to know," she whispered. "I had to know. So I went back to work at the Manor again. I worked there for years, at least five, maybe more, until the night I saw my gran's ghost." I watched in horror as a tear rolled down the deep lines of her face.

"Gran only said one thing, 'destroy the witch and free us'. I screamed and ran out of the Manor, never to return again." She lowered her chin to her chest and let out a dry, raspy sob. "My gran is still there. I left her to her fate. I left them all. I have spent the last sixty years trying to find out all I could about ghosts. I have talked to many people, questioning how to vanquish a witch's curse.

"Most of them laughed at me, called me a fool." She shook her head. " I was no fool. I was a desperate woman that wanted to free my kin. The kin I had left there so many years ago, knowing she was in torment. By the time I found someone that knew how to get rid of the witch, I was too old to do anything about it. I have sat here in my chair, wasting away, with this burden heavy on my heart."

I glanced over at Moira, who was looking at her gran with sadness, but I could tell she didn't believe it. It would be difficult for anyone to believe the stories, I supposed, unless you had witnessed the screams and whispers. "What is it?" my voice barely above a whisper as I turned back to the old woman. When she slowly turned those watery eyes back to mine, I elaborated. "How can I help them and break the curse?"

"Lacey..." Moira began to interrupt as her gran held her gnarled hands out to me. I set my forgotten cup next to hers and took both of her hands in mine. They felt as frail as they looked. The skin was papery thin, bluish-green veins visible and raised on the surface, her bones small and gnarled with large knuckles spotted from age. "Gran, that is enough. You've told your story. Now it is time for Lacey to go." Her voice was stern, but she quieted immediately when the old lady turned to her and fixed her with a glare that spoke volumes without saying anything at all.

She didn't say a word until she turned back to me. "Ye must find the bones. The witch's bones. Ye must find them and cover them with salt. Then light them on fire. They must burn, and then ye will send her to hell, where she belongs."

My mind was racing with the implications of completing such a task. How would I find them? Where could they be? If I did find them, how would I get away with digging up an old grave? I started to shake my head in denial, but she squeezed my fingers roughly.

"Ye must find her grave, dig it up, and salt the bones. They must burn."

I tried to pull my hands back, but her grip was stronger than it had any right to be at her age. I shook my head again. "I can't!" I cried out.

"Ye must!" Her voice cracked as she raised it. "Ye are the only one that can. Those people must be released. All of them!"

I tried to pull harder. At first, I hadn't wanted to hurt her by being too rough, but now I was scared. I was scared of her, and I was scared of what she was telling me I needed to do. Her grip seemed unnaturally strong and she wouldn't release me. I could feel my bones grinding and twisting under her tight grasp. Moira stood up and wrung her hands in front of her. I pleaded with the old woman. "Someone else…"

"Ye! Ye must salt bones and light them on fire until she is gone." She yanked me closer until I was practically falling over sideways in the chair. "Find the bones. Salt the bones. Burn the bones. Find the bones. Salt the bones. Burn the bones. Find the bones! Salt the bones! Burn the bones!"

She was practically screaming the words, her eyes manic. Spittle was flying from her mouth as she repeated herself over and over. All I could do was cry out pleas for her to let me go. Moira finally reached forward and began to pry the woman's bony fingers from where they were digging painfully into mine.

As soon as I was able to, I pulled free and jumped out of the chair, nearly knocking it over. "I have to go!" I cried out and spun towards the door that we had come in, running through the cottage, not seeing anything other than the desire to get away. The entire way to the door I could still hear her screaming. "Find the bones! Salt the bones! Burn the bones!"

I ran outside, ignoring the beautiful flower beds overflowing with colorful blooms, and swiped at my cheeks to wipe away the tears that were streaming down my face. I was almost to the walkway in front of the house when I heard a door slam behind me and whirled around to see Moira stalk towards me with a thunderous look on her face.

"I'm sorry!" I cried. "I didn't know!"

"Never come back here! Do ye hear me, girl?" Her anger laced every word, and all I could do was nod frantically. I never wanted to step foot inside again.

"I won't. I promise."

I turned around and ran back to the library where Doogal had dropped me off and prayed to all the gods that he was still there. If he wasn't, I would just have to walk back. It couldn't be more than a half-hour walk. Anything to get away from here. All I wanted was to curl up in my bed and sleep. The thought of the way Ian had comforted me and made me feel safe the night before spurred me on.

When I came around the corner, I breathed out a sigh of relief and slowed my pace, quickly wiping any remaining tears from my cheeks and chin. I knew I looked like a mess, even with a dry face. There was no hiding the emotional wreck I was. I could only hope that he would ignore it the way my dad used to pretend he didn't see my attacks.

Eleven

We rode back to the Manor in a comfortable silence, Doogal's companionable presence reassuring me from the front seat. By the time Doogal was pulling the car to a stop in front of the Manor, I was already starting to feel better. I smiled at him gratefully, to thank him for the ride, but to also thank him for not asking any questions.

I quickly made my way inside and up the stairs to my room, hoping to avoid anyone. I was still feeling too raw and vulnerable to have a polite conversation. As soon as the door shut behind me, I closed my eyes and leaned against it.

"What am I going to do?" I whispered, my voice fading away into the silence. At that moment, I had probably felt the most lonely that I had ever felt in my entire life. As I stood there with my head against the door, only one person came to mind that I wanted to keep me company and to just... be in my space. "Ian?"

Like before, my whisper faded away into nothingness. No one was around to hear it, and no one appeared like a genie being summoned from their bottle.

"Stupid, stupid, stupid. What did you think would happen, anyway? He'd probably show up just to warn you away from hurting his family again." I pushed away from the door and angrily brushed at my eyes, pushing my hair back from my face and swiping away any evidence that I was hurt. Ian wasn't my lap dog to come when I called. He probably couldn't hear me call at all, he was a ghost. There was no reason to be upset that he didn't answer when I needed him.

I stomped into the bathroom after toeing off my ballet flats and eyed the bathtub as I skirted around it like it would jump out and bite me. There wasn't much I would like more than to relax in a steaming hot bubble bath and relax away my stress, but after the whole witch trying to drown me incident, I'd been put off baths, so that was a big nope. Maybe when all the ghost business was resolved. No, not the ghosts. They obviously weren't dangerous. They only wanted to be free.

My shoulders slumped at the thought. Someone needed to help them. I couldn't back out, leaving them to remain in whatever sort of limbo they were trapped in. That would make *me* the monster. Tomorrow was my day off from teaching Olivia. I would spend the day in the local cemetery searching for a grave.

There was a rush of mixed emotions at the thought. Happiness to make a firm decision, dread at how it would go. I wouldn't address the increasing regret that *all* the ghosts would be released. I was also scared to death that I would find her grave, while also afraid I wouldn't and then not know what to do next. Maybe if I had the journals, they would tell me where the grave was. Another reason I needed to talk to Ian. While I still could.

Nope, not going to think of him that way. I turned on the water in the shower and started to strip off my clothes. I couldn't take a bath like I really longed to do, but I could let the hot water pound onto my stiff muscles in the shower. I was about to step in when I heard his voice. I squealed and spun to find him casually leaning against the door frame, and I frantically grabbed for a towel to cover my nakedness.

"*I felt... a pull.*" He stepped through the doorway and eyed my half-covered body, barely concealed by the fluffy white towel. His eyes raised to meet mine, his mossy green eyes heated and one eyebrow cocked. "*Was that because of you?*"

I swallowed as I watched his slow steps bring him closer. I nodded once shakily as he reached me. "Yes," I stopped to clear my throat. "Yes."

It was barely loud enough to hear over the spray of the water, but his expression turned concerned while he took in the look on my face.

I knew it was still blotchy from crying earlier and the flush that always happened when my anxiety took over. He reached out a hand like he had done in the conservatory and ran a thumb over the side of my face, down my jaw, and cupped me there. I gasped at the firm feeling of his hand on my skin.

"What happened?" His voice was gruff, but it was laced with concern as his eyes darted over my face, not seeming surprised that he was actually touching me. *Really* touching me.

"I spoke with someone from the village today. An older l-lady. She used to work here when she was a girl." I stopped to take a deeper breath as I let out everything to this man, this *ghost* that I was beginning to feel such a strong connection with that he was the first, the only person I wanted when I was distraught. "Her gran was k-killed by the witch. She researched how to destroy the witch her whole life and finally found the answer."

"And what is the answer, darling?"

I blinked rapidly, the mix of his soft tone and the returning fear making the emotions rise back to the surface. "She told me that I need to find Elspeth's grave. I need to dig it up and salt her bones before lighting them on fire. Burning her bones will banish her and will set free all the ghosts of the people she murdered." I swallowed hard and looked down from his eyes, staring at his chin and noticing the stubble that was dotted there, as if he hadn't shaved the day he died. "You will be set free."

When he didn't say anything in response to my words, I glanced back up to see him with a strange look on his face that I couldn't decipher. It could have been frustration or confusion, but his expression cleared before I could determine what it was. His eyes met mine again as he brought his other hand up as he used both hands to cup my face.

"What is it about you, Lacey?" All I could do was shake my head, since I didn't have an answer for him. He ran a thumb over my bottom lip lightly before pulling it gently down. *"I'm going to kiss you now."*

It was all the warning he gave me before he lowered his head, using his hold on my chin to tilt my face up to meet his. The press of his mouth against mine was light at first, leaving me wanting so much more. It was my first kiss from a man other than the rare cheek kisses my father bestowed on me. My breath froze in my lungs at the faintly warm feel of him. He wasn't as warm as a person would normally feel, I realized. He was there, but also wasn't. But the kiss was real.

He quickly took it from a light pressing of the lips to so much more in a flash of time. He tilted my head to allow better access and firmly fit his mouth across mine. We both moaned at the feeling of it just being *right* to have him there, kissing me. My towel was forgotten as I lifted both hands to place them around his neck. I could barely reach, having to rise on my toes to fit myself properly against him.

His lips spread, coaxing mine to do the same. *"Open for me,* mo ghràidh,*"* his Scottish brogue was deeper than I had heard from him, making shivers skate across my flesh as I did what he demanded. As soon as I opened my lips, his tongue swept over my bottom lip. He swiped over my tongue, and I whimpered with a need I didn't understand, but my body clearly did.

My naked breasts rubbed against his shirt, making the already hardened peaks tingle with a delicious need that warmed my belly. The kiss went on and on, his tongue stroking mine, making me lose any thought until I could only need.

He drew back with a groan and rested his forehead against mine, both of us breathing heavily in the small space between us.

"My darling, I need you to take your shower now, okay?"

I opened my eyes to look up at him, my hurt at his words dissipating at the look on his face. He looked like a man that was in pain. "Are you okay?" My whisper made him groan as he slowly pulled his hands away from me. He waited until I was steady on my feet before stepping back. His eyes darkened as they took in my nakedness, flushed with arousal. I grew even more heated, this time with embarrassment, and bent down to pick the towel at my feet back up to hold over my pebbled nipples, hiding my body once again.

"No, darling, I am not okay. But if I gave in to what my body wants to do to yours, you wouldn't be either. You aren't ready for that, though, are you?" That damned eyebrow lifted again as a lopsided, cocky grin

took over his handsome face. Ugh, but why did that cockiness turn me on even more than the sweet side of him?

Was I ready for what he was insinuating? I didn't know if it was even possible. I mean, he was a ghost, and I was... not. But he was mostly solid now. He could touch me, and I could feel it. I supposed that meant sex with him could very, very easily happen.

His chuckle startled me out of my thoughts. *"Oh, Lacey, the fact that you are thinking so hard about it tells me that, no, you are not ready for what I want to do to your delicate little body. Take your shower. I will wait in your room. When you are done, we will discuss this grave digging business more thoroughly."*

He turned around and walked out of the bathroom before I could respond. I was irritated at his humor at my expense, but I also had to be thankful for his thoughtfulness. He would have been able to get into me with little to no pressure a few minutes ago, but now that my thoughts were clearer, I knew he was right. I was not ready... yet.

I could easily see myself giving myself to him. I had never felt this way for anyone before, having been raised unconventionally due to my anxiety issues. Going to college was hard for me on a day-to-day basis and didn't allow me to let anyone close enough to even make proper friends, let alone a boyfriend. Jumping into bed with a ghost I had only spoken to a handful of times, no matter the connection we seemed to have, was a step so far out of my comfort zone, I didn't know when I would be able to make that decision on my own.

I stepped into the shower and let the water sluice over me. If I led the way on my timeframe, it could take months or even years to break past the barrier my anxiety was sure to always throw up. I was beginning to think that what I really needed was to just give over all the decisions to him. He was proving to have my well-being in mind. He wasn't rushing me. For that, I was so grateful and led me to want to trust him fully.

The whispers started while I was rinsing the conditioner out of my hair. As usual, they were mostly indistinct, with so many voices overlapping. I could make out words here and there, but the meaning was clear. The ghosts were desperate to be freed. I knew they weren't going to stop begging. Somehow, my arrival had started something, and I didn't know how to explain it. I didn't know why I was involved at all, let alone seeming to be the one person in all the years to come along capable of breaking the curse that held them.

I thought of Elspeth's rooms. The journal said she wrote things on her walls. I wondered if there was a clue there. I had to have somewhere to start looking. Tomorrow, before I headed to the cemetery, I would go into her wing and have a look around the space.

An angry scream sounded right behind me, making me startle and spin around. Elspeth was right there in front of me, her stringy hair waving around her in a wind that I couldn't feel just like it had while in the castle ruins. Her tattered dress wrapped around her as the water from the shower went straight through her incorporeal form. She shrieked again, and I gasped, jumping back, slipping on the wet tile, and falling to the floor just as she reached out towards me, her chipped and jagged fingernails swiping through the air where I had stood.

I screamed as I curled into a ball on the floor of the shower, my hands covering my head. Suddenly, the air got colder as the door was flung open and Ian stepped in with a growl. Keeping myself huddled in a ball with my eyes shut tight, I couldn't see what was happening, but I could hear his grunts and her angry screams, then finally silence.

I felt a hand touch my shoulder, and I jerked, another scream rising before dying quickly as Ian whispered softly to me. He turned the water off and then covered me in a thick towel before lifting me from the cold floor. I turned to grip his shoulders tightly and tucked my face against his neck.

He continued to whisper quietly to me as he carried me to the bed and tucked me in, pulling the wet towel out from under me and pulling the blankets over my shaking body. I thought he was leaving me and started to call out for him, but when I opened my eyes to search for him, I saw him removing his wet clothes. There were deep scratch marks on his arms, and I wanted to cry for him. For the danger he put himself in to protect me.

He slid into the bed with me and pulled me close, hushing me as he kissed my head and held me against his hard body.

"*I've got you,* mo ghràidh. *I will keep you safe, always.*"

With him wrapped around me, I fell into a deep sleep.

Twelve

When I woke up, I was alone, just like I had been the last time he had watched over me in my sleep. I dropped back down onto my pillow with a disappointed huff and then winced at the small aches I felt. I dragged myself out of the bed and padded into the bathroom to investigate, turning sideways to see my shoulder and hip in the mirror.

There were two small bruises from where I had fallen against the shower floor and wall. I lifted my hand to gently probe at a sore spot on my head. It wasn't bad, just a bit tender. I knew it could have been so much worse. I shuddered at the memory of the witch reaching for me. That was a memory I could do without. I also couldn't help but wonder what Ian did to get her to go away again. That was the second time he had fought her for me. Maybe the third, I thought as I looked at the bathtub and remembered how he kept her from drowning me.

I had a ghost working overtime to keep me from becoming a ghost by another ghost. If my parents knew what I was going through here, they would have me on the next flight out. I thought of my mother, with guilt flooding me. I would need to call her today. I couldn't keep texting her, she would need to hear my voice, or she would begin to worry about me.

I hesitated, but stepped into the shower, letting the water wash over me. I was starting to get pissed off that my bathing time kept getting interrupted. Even though all the voices were quiet for once, I washed as quickly as possible, not wanting to delay any longer than necessary and hoping that I wouldn't be caught off guard again.

There was one presence I did miss. All through my shower and getting dressed in a pair of jeans and a simple long sleeve cotton shirt, I thought of Ian and wondered where he went when he wasn't here. I hoped that wherever his soul was; it wasn't in pain. What exactly did it mean to be in limbo? I could imagine it was awful.

I brushed my hair back and wrapped it up into a bun on top of my head, and slipped on my flats. I needed to head down to the kitchen and find out what Isla's plans were for the day. I also needed to talk to her about exploring Elsbeth's rooms. Just the thought of entering her space had a shiver of dread racing up my spine.

As I reached for the doorknob, I hung my head and blew out a few calming breaths to steady myself. All I could do was keep reassuring myself that I was strong and that I could do this. I straightened my shoulders and raised my head high, determined to get through whatever was to come.

As my steps drew nearer the kitchen, I could hear the giggles of Olivia, and it immediately brightened my mood.

"Good morning, ladies!" I called out and stopped behind Olivia's chair to place a light kiss on the top of her head. "What are your plans for your day together?" Isla had mentioned during my interview process that every Saturday, she and Olivia had a girl's day together. It sounded wonderful, and when, or if, I ever had my own child, it was something I think I would enjoy as well.

"We are going to the city to have our nails done and do a bit of shopping," Isla answered with a smile as I popped a coffee pod in the machine and hit the brew button.

"That sounds lovely." I smiled over at Olivia, who was practically vibrating in her seat with excitement. "Do you know what color you want on your nails, sweetheart?"

"Rainbow!" she shouted, holding up her hands. "I want a different color on every nail. It will be so pretty!"

I grinned. "It will be perfect, just like you," giving her a wink as I finished doctoring my coffee. Raising the cup to my lips, I blew on it a little before braving a small sip and turning to Isla. "I was wondering if I could explore the Manor a bit today? Are there any rooms off-limits that I should know about? Other than your private rooms, of course."

She looked at me with a tilt of her head, and I tried to smile back, but I was sure it came out more like a grimace. I could never hide anything from my parents, and though Isla was closer to my age, only about ten years older than me, her position as my employer gave me the same kind of feelings that I had when I tried to hide my guilt.

"Not really," she started, still giving me her quizzical look. "There is an older section in the west wing that has been closed up for decades. I don't mind if you poke around in there. Just make sure you are careful when you go in." Yep, she was on to me. I blew out a breath and nodded.

"Of course. Thank you."

She nodded back, giving me a look that I interpreted as we would be having a conversation about this later when little ears weren't present. Shit. I hoped she wasn't upset at me for springing it on her when she couldn't say more.

She stood up and gathered their plates and cups. "Well, honey bear, we should get moving if we want to make our appointment with Miss Cathy."

"Okay, mam!" Olivia climbed to her feet and grabbed her crutches. "Are you going to have fun today, too, Miss Lacey?"

Internally I shuddered, thinking of all the fun I was *not* going to have while exploring a witch's rooms, but I smiled for her. "I hope so!" She came around the table to give me a hug, and I held on to her, absorbing her warmth and light. "You have a good day with your mother, okay, sweetheart?"

"We will! Bye!"

"Bye, Lacey. Be careful exploring." Isla placed her hand on Olivia's back and guided her toward the door.

"I will," I said quietly, the guilt filling me again. "Thank you."

She nodded once, and they were gone as I sat there at the family table, staring into my rapidly cooling coffee. It was during moments like this that I felt truly isolated and very, very lonely. I was used to being alone, but that didn't mean that I liked it. I was comfortable with my own presence and didn't need someone to keep me company, but that didn't mean I didn't ache for someone special to spend my time with.

My mind drifted back to Ian as I stared out the window to where I could see the rocky cliffs and the angry waves crashing far below the Manor. I wondered, had he still been alive, would Isla have hired me? Would I have met him, and would he have been interested in his niece's quiet and awkward teacher? I wish I knew the answer to those questions. Knowing that he was no longer alive and that whatever we had now could never last had a sadness pressing down on me so strongly that I wanted to lower my head to my arms on the table and weep.

I was feeling a loss for something I never had to begin with, and it hurt so badly. I thought of our kiss last night and decided then that if he wanted to take our relationship, such as it were, to the next level, I wouldn't overthink it. Life was short, and if I let him go without ever experiencing the passion I felt in his arms again, even for a fleeting moment in time, I would regret it for the rest of my life. And if the witch had any say in it, that life would be pretty damn short.

I picked up my cup and drank the last of my coffee before standing and taking it to the sink. I grabbed a couple of slices of toast that were leftover from the breakfast Isla had made and left the room, knowing there was a staff member that was responsible for cleaning up. I was still getting used to the idea of having housekeepers doing the dishes and washing my laundry.

I stopped in the middle of the floor in the great hall and eyed the stairs that I knew would lead to the west wing. I took a bite of my toast as I contemplated what I would find when I was up there. Nothing good, I was sure. The toast went down like sandpaper in my throat, and I swallowed hard.

Finally, I took the first step needed to reach the west wing. Then the next. I was dragging my feet, and I knew it. Searching the rooms wasn't my only plan for the day. I also needed to make a trip to the local cemetery. I glanced toward the front door and thought about heading there first, but that would just be putting off the inevitable.

So up the stairs I went, trailing my hand along the railing as I nibbled on my toast. Once I reached the top, I turned to the left, not knowing exactly where I was going, but figured I would know once I found it. If Elspeth were put in the furthest rooms in the huge Manor, it stood to reason that I would head that way.

I nodded cordially to a member of the house staff that was polishing a large vase on a beautiful table with gleaming wood. We exchanged a couple of pleasantries as I continued past. It had seemed strange to me since the very beginning that I rarely saw the staff about, yet everything was always polished to a gleaming shine and smelled like citrus. I wondered if they kept Elspeth's rooms just as clean as I held my hand under the last bit of my toast as I finished it off, careful not to drop any crumbs.

I turned down the furthest hallway and paused, a sinister feeling of dread swept over me. I was certain that I had arrived at the correct place. I wasn't sure if it was just my mind playing with me, like when I was a little girl ready to turn out my bedroom light and had a flash of fear that there might be a boogeyman waiting for me in the closet or under my bed ready to reach out and grab me. Or if the feeling was a by-product of the witch's presence from either now or in the past when she used to walk these halls.

I was grateful that the whispers had been absent during my trek to these rooms. I didn't know if I would have maintained the courage to see this through had I been followed by ghosts.

I stopped in front of the furthest door and clenched my hands at my side while I had a pep talk with myself. I could do this. No one was here. It was only a quick look around. Likely, there wasn't even anything to see in the empty rooms.

Finally, I reached out with a trembling hand and rested it on the doorknob, ignoring the spike of fear that nearly had me bolting back out of the wing and into the conservatory, where Isla had convinced me I would feel safe. I quickly jerked the knob, and the door pushed open on creaky hinges. *Great*, as if anything needed to be added to the overall spooky ambiance.

Before I even stepped into the room, I could tell it hadn't been entered in a very long time, by anyone human at least. The first thing I noticed was the musty smell of a long-time closed room. It was very dim inside, even though there were several large windows lining the outside wall. They were covered in long, dark, heavy drapes, not fully closed but not opened far enough to offer much natural light into the room. I looked for a switch along the wall next to me, but stopped looking once I noticed the walls were filthy.

I quickly pulled my cell phone from the back pocket of my jeans and turned the flashlight function on, aiming it toward the wall closest to me. A breath caught in my throat, making me choke on the stale air.

"What the hell..."

The wallpaper was shredded by what looked to be a jagged object deep enough to gouge the wood beneath. I stepped further in and closer to the wall to study it. I couldn't tell if what I was seeing was just scribbles from a mad mind or if there was a method to the madness.

There were lines and circles. What looked like scribbles marked the shredded paper as well as the wood. It was made with something dark. I couldn't stop myself from stepping up to the wall and lifting a hand to swipe a finger through one of the lines. I jerked back at the contact with the substance.

An electric jolt ran through me at the touch, along with a heavy dose of fear. The lines and what could have been symbols gave off an eerie, sinister vibe, and for the first time, I truly regretted stepping foot into the room. I eyed the door as I brought my finger into the light, debating on running like the hounds of hell were on my heels.

I glanced down at the smudge on my finger and stared at it. It looked ashy and felt gritty as I rubbed my fingers together. I glanced toward the fireplace against the wall, past the sitting chairs that were likely elegant at one time, but were now dark and faded with age. They looked to be covered in whatever was on the walls and my hand. Soot. It had to be soot from the fireplace.

I walked around the chairs and over a piece of broken wood that was probably a small end table, making my way over to the fireplace as if I were being drawn there. Why I needed to see it, I had no idea, all I knew was that I did. It was a compulsion I was helpless to resist. Before I made it there, I swept my light around the room in front of me. There were no picture frames. No vases for flowers or pottery from statues or nicknacks. Nothing but empty space, and I knew it wasn't because they had been packed away after her death.

I shone the light into the fireplace and gasped. There, mixed in with ashes from long ago, were the missing journals. Only, they weren't as I had last seen them. They were shredded to pieces, and what remained of them was burnt to an unreadable mess.

Thirteen

I spun around and swept my light wildly back and forth in front of me as my mind raced. I didn't know how she could have destroyed the journals, but I couldn't fathom anyone in the house doing it either. The room didn't smell of fresh burnt paper the way I would have guessed it would if it had been done recently. The room looked undisturbed, and I truly believed that I was the first to enter in a very long time.

The light drew my eyes to the windows, and I slowly made my way to the half-closed drapes. I pulled aside one of the panels to see that the glass was coated in a thin film of grime. I tilted my head and studied the window until it hit me. The windows had been replaced sometime in the last few decades. Likely when the rest of the house had been updated, they hadn't forgotten to do these rooms as well, but that seemed to be the only thing that had been changed in nearly two hundred years.

I let the drape drop back into place, dust flying out from it, and I waved my hand in front of my face to keep it back as I coughed a few times. I glanced back at the destroyed books in the fireplace and wanted to cry at the loss of a piece of history. Now no one would ever be able to read about Colleen and her life, how she loved husband and son. Any answers to the questions I had hoped would be answered in them were gone as well. Burnt to ashes. The same ashes that were scrawled on every wall in these depressing rooms. My disappointment lingered heavily in the air, adding to the gloomy atmosphere of the room.

I stepped over and around broken furniture, perking up a bit when I spied an open door to what I assumed was the bedchamber. I let the open door beckon me forward, needing to complete my inspection of the rooms of the woman that had tormented every generation that had come after her. They were her descendants, but she had treated them as if they were her enemies, and I needed to know why.

Was she really so caught up in unfounded jealousy? Had she hated her life here in this opulent mansion so much? I knew that she had been forced into the arranged marriage as most brides of that time were, but so had Colleen. There was a major difference between their lives, though. Colleen had embraced her life and accepted that the man she was going to marry was hers as much as she was his. She found a way to be happy. Elspeth seemed to hate everything about her marriage and life here at the Manor.

I thought about the maid that I had been told about, the one that Elspeth had caught her husband comforting. Had that been the turning point in her life of hatred, or was it just an excuse? Was he having an affair? Could I blame him for finding love when the woman he had been given to share his life with was so awful?

I shook my head. I couldn't judge how someone would react, but I could judge how their actions hurt innocent people. Innocents like Olivia. Would she be murdered eventually as well? Like Ian. *Oh, Ian.*

As if my thoughts had conjured him, the air rippled next to me as I stood just outside the bedchamber. My hand flew to my throat as a scream caught in my throat.

"Lacey, are you okay?" His words drifted away as he took a look around until his eyes came back to me, a mix of anger and concern filling their green depths. *"What are you doing in here, Lacey?"*

I shook my head, my heart racing uncontrollably, my words stuck in my throat as I took several deep gasps of air. He immediately looked contrite and reached out for my face.

"*Breathe, darling. It's okay. It's okay.*" I nodded and took my first deep, lung-filling breath.

"The journals. They disappeared." I looked at him with pleading eyes. "I had to see if I could find some answers here. Especially after what happened yesterday."

"*And what have you found, other than destroyed and decaying rooms that have been locked and forbidden for more than a century?*"

I gave him a confused look. "They weren't locked."

"*Of course they were. I am the only one with a key. The same as my father before me.*"

"But..." I looked around, seeing the destruction, before facing him again. "Isla gave me permission to look around.

He looked frustrated as he cupped my cheek with one of his hands and placed the other on one of my hips. "*Darling, Isla had no idea the rooms were locked. As a child, she never had any interest in seeking out the witch. She was warned from coming up here, just like everyone else. She wouldn't have had the key to open it for you in any case, since the key is well hidden from everyone.*"

His words had all the fine hairs on my body standing on end. "Then h-how was the door unlocked?"

He shook his head as his eyes bore into mine, concern clouding them as he stared at me. "*I don't know, but you shouldn't be here.*"

At his words, the most bone-chilling laugh I could have ever imagined filled the rooms. I jumped, and we both whirled around to face the witch, his arms going protectively around me, but she was nowhere to be seen. The haunting cackle echoed off the walls, making it impossible to discern where it was coming from. I felt him tug on my hand, breaking me from my frozen state of shock.

"*Come on, let's go.*" He started pulling me quickly back towards the open door that led out of the rooms. I tripped over something I couldn't see, but he yanked me up hard, practically dragging me. Just as we were about to reach the door, it swung closed with a loud bang, startling a scream out of me.

Ian immediately tried pulling the door back open, but it wouldn't budge. He let my hand go and threw his weight against the door in a futile attempt to make it open, then punched it with his fist before growling. He cursed in frustration and turned back to the open bedroom door.

"There's another door in the bedroom. We have to try it," he growled, immediately grabbing my hand again and pulling me back across the floor, kicking aside anything that could trip me. The laughing just grew louder and seemed to grow in intensity. I couldn't hold back the sob that had been building in my throat as I had watched him tackle the door.

As we went through the doorway, I didn't have much time to look around, barely noticing the made bed and tattered curtains hanging in the corners of the tall four posters. The door was closed, of course, but as soon as I saw it, hope bloomed in my chest. It quickly died as he tried to turn the knob, and it wouldn't budge.

"What are we going to do?" I cried, panic quickly taking hold of me and squeezing tight.

Ian turned to me, his eyes wild but determined. *"I will get you out of here, Lacey. I won't let her harm you. Trust me on that."*

He turned around and surveyed the room, his eyes sweeping over the tables and cursing. He strode to the four-poster bed and kicked one of the posts several times until it cracked loudly, breaking from its place. He gave a vicious twist, freeing it and, using it like a bat, swung it at the doorknob.

As I watched him take several swings, making wood splinters fly with every hit, I began to notice a smell. It grew stronger by the second, until I had to pull my shirt up over my nose to stop from gagging.

"What the hell is that smell?" As much as I didn't want to, I turned to see what was behind me. It took me a minute to locate the cause, but when I did, I screamed, terror clawing at me. I watched, horrified, as the dead, decaying body laying on the once empty bed turned its head to look at me. Elspeth's corpse opened its mouth and screamed back at me. The shriek was so loud I had to cover my ears and wince with the pain it caused.

"Why are you doing this?" I pleaded desperately as Ian never once paused in his hammering of the door. "They're your family! The children of your own child!"

The white, filmy dead eyes of her corpse narrowed, and I could have sworn I saw true hatred fill their empty depths. It had been the wrong thing to say. She slowly sat up and swung her legs over the side of the bed as her hatred zeroed in on me.

I stumbled backward, bumping into the wall hard. "Ian!" He turned at my scream, and his eyes widened when he caught sight of the witch pushing herself to her feet. The rotting corpse stumbled sideways before catching herself on the splintered post. The broken wood dug into her flesh, tearing it, making it ooze thick, black, tar-like blood. It also made the stench intensify, causing me to gag hard enough that I was afraid I would vomit. It was the worst thing I had ever smelled in my life, and I hoped I would never have to face it again.

Elspeth looked down at her bleeding hand, and her face contorted into a fierce scowl before looking back at me in rage. She stumbled forward, her arms outstretched, reaching for me.

"Ian!" I screamed again, just as there was a metallic clank, and the doorknob he had been hammering on fell to the floor.

"*Hang on,*" he grunted, prying at the edge of the door with both hands, slowly pulling it open. I could see it giving way, but I didn't dare take my eyes off Elspeth for long.

She was just a few feet away, her clawed fingertips reaching for me when the door swung open wide, and Ian pulled me through. Before he had me through the doorway, though, she grabbed the top of my arm with both of her hands and yanked me roughly back towards her.

I was caught between a tug-of-war with Ian desperately trying to pull me to safety, and the long dead corpse of Elspeth Campbell trying to keep me in her room. I was scared to death of what would happen to me if I ended up locked in there with her. I knew I would never come out alive again. Death wasn't what I was afraid of, though. It was whatever she had planned for me.

Tears were streaming down my face, and I was sobbing uncontrollably as I yanked hard against her hold. All of a sudden, I saw a fist fly past my face and into the corpse, making a sickening squelching sound as it landed against her cheekbone. It was enough of a distraction for her to lose her hold on me, and I went flying backward with the momentum, banging my head viciously on the doorjamb.

We landed in a heap on the floor, both of us breathing heavily. Ian gathered me in his arms and lay his cheek on my head as I continued to sob, though my cries had turned into relief rather than the terror-filled ones of just a minute ago.

Just as I sank into Ian's arms, relieved that the nightmare was finally over, an enormous crash startled me. I turned my head back to the door and watched in stunned disbelief as the door bowed outward as it was hit from the other side. Then, as what sounded like fists hitting the wood began, I could literally see where each blow landed against the door. With every bang of her fist, the door continued to bow in that spot, a perfect, round shape, before retreating back to normal.

I reached backward blindly, trying to find Ian's hand, needing his grip to hold me steady and to ground me in reality. What I was seeing was not possible.

"How is she doing this?" I whispered, not really expecting an answer. There were no logical answers for anything that had to do with Elspeth. One thing was certain: she was a monster and needed to be stopped.

"Come on. We need to get you cleaned up."

Ian helped me to my feet, and we walked away as the pounding on the door continued, the witch's shrieks following us down the hall and away from the west wing.

Fourteen

I hissed in a breath as Ian dabbed at my temple with a wet cloth.
"*You banged your head pretty good, darling,*" he tsked as he rinsed the cloth again. I watched as the red swirled down the drain of the sink, my blood standing out starkly against the bright white porcelain. "*I want you to go into town and get looked at by Dr. Ewan. He's a good man, gentle with his hands. He's also good at making his patients laugh. We had to take little Olivia a few months ago when she cut her hand. He had her smiling and laughing even as he glued and bandaged her up.*"

He stopped his movements for a moment, and I looked up into his face from my perch on the bathroom counter to see the sadness there. I raised my hand and cupped his cheek, watching as he closed his eyes against the pain of losing his only family.

When he opened his eyes back up, I leaned forward and lightly pressed my lips against his and just whispered, "Okay."

He dropped the cloth in the sink and pulled me tight against his chest. His lips met mine again, but this time it wasn't soft and gentle. It was no light peck. It was a full assault on my mouth. Lips, teeth, and tongue all worked together to drive both of us into a passionate frenzy.

It wasn't until he gripped my hair tightly to tip my head back further that I cried out with the sudden pain, and he pulled away to curse viciously.

We were both breathing heavily as he let go of my hair and gently stroked it, laying his forehead against mine with his eyes closed. We sat there for a long time, just breathing each other in, when he finally broke the silence.

"I thought I was going to lose you. I thought I was going to fail the promise I made to you." He looked at the cut on my temple and swore again before reaching for the cloth and wiping away the new blood that had begun dripping. *"I did fail you. You are hurt. I wasn't able to protect you."*

I lifted my hand and placed it over his. "It's a head wound, Ian. They always bleed more. You *did* protect me. If it wasn't for you, I don't think I could have made it out of there." I shook my head ruefully and gave him a half smile. "I know I wouldn't have made it out. You didn't fail me. You saved me."

"I hate seeing you hurt. The thought of losing you when I just found you..." He looked at me with so much intensity I thought I would combust. *"You are mine, Lacey. Mine. As long as I am here with you."*

Those were the crucial words, though, weren't they? As much as I loved hearing him call me his, the knowledge that he wouldn't be here for long is what was killing me inside.

"Kiss me," I whispered, needing him to erase the ache that bloomed in my heart at the thought of him disappearing forever.

"I will kiss you gently, for now, darling. Once the good doctor patches you up and clears you, I promise to do so much more."

I swallowed hard at his words and stared into his handsome face. It was nearly solid, but not quite. It was strange seeing and touching this man, having him touch me, but being able to practically see through him. He was still a ghost, even if he could easily interact with the world around him. "Will you be able to come back when I'm done?"

He looked pained, a tortured look crossing his features. *"The truth is, I don't know."*

"How are you able to do the things you do? You aren't like the other ghosts..." I paused and glanced around my room, not really looking at anything, just trying to piece my thoughts together. "Where do you go when you leave? Why can you act normally when they seem trapped, I don't know, in a moment of time? It's obvious they are tortured souls desperately wanting to be released. It's so strange."

He ran a hand through his thick, dark hair, and frustration layered his voice. *"I wish I knew. I don't know where I go. It's just dark. Sometimes I think I can hear people talking and sounds... it doesn't make sense. Then there are times that I am so worried about my sister and niece."* He looked at me and placed his hand on my cheek. *"And you. I just want to see you so much, and then I'm here. I have no explanation for it. There have been a couple of times, like the other night and today, that I felt your need for me and allowed myself to be pulled to you."*

I smiled softly, even though my heart ached at his pain. "I'm glad you're here, Ian. I don't think I could have done any of this without you." My eyes welled up, and I tried blinking away the tears. I had spent enough time with this man to know that he was important to me on a level I barely understood. And I was going to lose him one day soon. It was awful, the feeling of knowing that I was going to lose him when I barely had him. Life would never be the same.

He swiped his thumb over the tear I couldn't hold back and leaned in to whisper a kiss over my lips. *"Promise me something, okay, darling?"* I sniffled and nodded my agreement, knowing I would agree to just about anything he asked of me. *"Don't think about tomorrow. Focus on right now, here, today. The only thing that matters is what we have in this moment. Promise me."*

Again, I nodded. It was all I could do because if I were to focus on the future without him in it, holding me like this a year from now, twenty? I wouldn't be able to function.

"Good." He kissed me again and brought me to my feet, waiting until I was steady, and handed me the cloth to hold to my still weeping wound. *"Now, go to Dr. Ewen and let him patch you up. If I have any say in the matter at all, I will be here when you get back."*

I sighed and pressed the damp cloth to my head before standing on my toes to give him one last kiss against the short stubble on his jaw. "Okay, Ian."

I pulled my phone out of my pocket to call Doogal and noticed I had several messages and a missed call from my mom. I winced, immediately feeling guilty. So much had been happening since I arrived that I barely gave her much thought. It wasn't fair to her. I vowed to call her as soon as I called Doogal for a ride.

He agreed to meet me out front in just a few minutes, so I hit my mother's contact as Ian watched on with his arms crossed over his broad chest. I was so busy staring at the veins in his forearms that I missed my mother saying hello, and she had to call my name twice before I jerked my eyes away, just to see him smirk at me. I gave him a mock glare and turned away, walking towards my bedroom door.

"I'm here, mom. Sorry, I was distracted by something for just a minute there."

As I walked out the door, I couldn't resist turning back one more time and saw Ian with a look on his face that could easily be interpreted as longing. I gave a small wave and walked out the door before my feet could take me back to him.

As I made my way down the hall and stairs, I listened as my mother told me how worried she had been and apologized several times, using Olivia as an excuse for my delay in calling her back, wincing at the lie. There was no way I could tell her anything. I couldn't imagine what she would think of my experience in the witch's quarters. Even remembering it made beads of cold sweat break out on my back and terror zing through my body. I thought of the corpse and hoped like hell that I would never see anything like that again.

"I promise, mom, everything is going great. I will take some pictures of the house and Olivia, so you can see how great I have it here. Trust me; you're going to be jealous. How are classes going?" The change of subject worked as I'd hoped, and she began telling me about all the young, brilliant minds that she was helping to shape. She was a great professor and loved her job, always had. My dad loved his job just as much, but he wasn't as enthusiastic as she was.

"Oh, sweetheart. Will you come back home for the holidays? Your father and I would love to see you."

I thought of going back into the bustling airport and being around all those people. Twice. A round-trip flight that would last more than twenty-four hours? I think I would rather take my chances with the witch. I shuddered. "Mom, I don't know. The flight..."

She sighed with understanding, but also sadness. "I know, sweetie, it's okay. Maybe your dad and I could come to see you. Are there any inns nearby? Or hotels. Hostels! Don't they call them hostels in other countries?"

I laughed. "I'm not sure, to be honest. Maybe? But there would be no need for that. This place has, like, a hundred rooms. I know Isla could spare one for you and dad."

"Oh, I don't want to intrude on her home."

"Mom, this is so much more than a home. If you saw it, you would understand."

I saw Doogal pulling the car around and knew I couldn't have my mom on the phone when he saw me. It was a sure thing that he would ask me about my injury, and that was a sure way to get Madison Conrad to freak out. "Hey, mom? I am so sorry, but I need to go. Can I call you later? I promise I will give you a call. No more radio silence from me, I swear."

"It's okay, sweetheart. My first class is about to start soon, so I need to go too. I love you, Lacey. So does dad."

"I love you, too. Give dad my love, okay?"

"Of course."

"Okay, bye!"

I hung up just as Doogal swung his door open and stepped out. His eyes narrowed on the cloth that was still pressed to my head. "Miss Lacey?"

I waved a hand around, trying to reassure him that it was no big deal. "It's just a tiny cut. You know how head wounds are. We thought it would be best to see the doctor just in case it might need a stitch or two."

"We?" He raised a bushy, graying red eyebrow and gave me a look. "Aren't Miss Isla and Miss Olivia gone for the day?"

I had to hide my panic and forced a smile on my face. "My mom!" I said a little too loudly and cleared my throat awkwardly. "I was on the phone with my mom and told her what happened. I slipped and bumped my head on the doorway. No big deal, but she convinced me to go to the doctor. So... that's where I'm going?" God, I hated lying, and it was always obvious when I was. The question at the end of my statement was proof of that.

He grunted but didn't press the issue further. He led me around the car to the passenger seat and helped me in. It was sweet, but I really felt fine, other than a bit of pain right at the area of the cut. I thought that maybe I grazed the wood pretty hard but didn't have a full impact against the doorframe. Thinking about the alternative of not being able to leave that room made me grateful for the injury.

Doogal pulled up outside a small building with a sign above the door stating that it was the doctor's office of Ewen McAllister. He assured me that he would wait regardless of how long the visit took, and I squeezed his hand in thanks.

"Get on with ye, Miss Lacey." His weathered face was red with embarrassment, and I couldn't help a small giggle as I got out of the car and waved to him before stepping through the door.

There were several empty seats. Only a young woman sat in one of the seats holding a baby no more than a few months old. I smiled at her as she waved and continued to bounce the adorable little boy with dimples on his cheeks and drool covering his chin.

I walked up to the window and looked for a clipboard or something to write my name down when a beautiful woman around my age walked through a doorway and smiled when she saw me. Her eyes immediately went to my head.

"Oh, my! I'm guessing you need to see the doctor right away!" She turned and rushed back through the doorway before I could protest, knowing that I'd be skipping in front of the woman and her baby.

I turned back to face the waiting room. The baby had been bouncing happily but was now eating noisily at his mother's breast.

"I'm sorry if they skip you to look at my head," I said, feeling mortified.

"No worries, hun. Brody won't want to stop until he's full anyway, or he'll be a little terror. It's best to get him fed." I nodded, grateful for the baby's appetite.

It wasn't a moment later that the beautiful woman opened the door and beckoned me through. "Come, let the doctor take a look at your head."

I swallowed and walked through the door, feeling my anxiety starting to rise now that I was going to be in a new environment.

Fifteen

The doctor was older than I had expected. He could have been my grandfather's age, but he was kind and gentle as he pulled the damp rag away and tsked at my cut. He hummed softly as he dabbed at it with a cotton pad he pulled out of a sealed package and glanced at my eyes when he squirted some saline on another.

I knew what he wanted and panicked a little inside. I hadn't prepared an excuse for my injury and had to think fast. I decided to go with the closest thing to the truth.

"I, um, banged my head against the doorframe." I felt my cheeks heat with the lie and just hoped that he would think it was from embarrassment instead of my guilt.

He hummed again and continued to dab at the cut. "Did the doorframe just jump out in front of you?"

My eyes darted up to his to see them twinkling with mirth. "No," I laughed a bit too stiffly as I tried to play it off. "I just wasn't watching where I was going."

He made that same humming noise in his throat that told me he wasn't buying my story. Not at all. When he started talking again, he had my full attention instantly.

"You know, my family have been the physicians of the Campbells since they settled here. About, oh, perhaps three hundred years or so. Well before the Manor was built. We were just called healers then."

"Oh, wow," I breathed out. As an American, it was difficult for me to imagine the length of time that other countries existed. Our country was still so young in comparison to others, and if we never left to explore the world, it was easy to forget that there was so much more to the world than our little corner of it.

"Yes. I think it was my great, great… great grandfather that was the healer for the Campbells that first lived in the Manor." He stood up, and I watched as he threw away his pile of paper and cotton pads. He went to a cabinet and pulled out a few more supplies. As he walked back to me, he held them up. "I don't believe you need any sutures. I'm going to tape you up, and you should be fine as long as you don't get them wet… or run into any more ghosts."

My eyes got wide as I stared at him, then my shoulders slumped. "How did you know?"

"That you were lying? My daughter used to act the same way whenever she was caught. Even if she were holding the evidence in her hand, she would turn red and try to come up with a plausible answer. It was rarely believable." He paused, set his hands down with all his supplies, and looked at me seriously, his knowing eyes studying me carefully. "I've also heard stories about what happens in that house, same as anyone else in this village."

I let out a breath I hadn't realized I had been holding and decided I should talk to him. I didn't know why. Maybe it was his demeanor. He seemed kind and sincerely cared about my well-being. Maybe it was his connection to the family, albeit distant.

"I've been hearing things. And seeing things." I admitted quietly.

"And being hurt by things?"

I nodded and started to lift my hand up to probe at my cut, but thought better of it since he had just cleaned it thoroughly. "Yes. She's tried to hurt me. A few times, actually."

He seemed surprised at my words. "That's unusual," he murmured. "She tends to either scare someone away or cause an accident."

My mouth flattened as I thought of Ian, her latest victim. "Kills them, you mean. I don't understand it!" I fumed, getting angry, thinking of what she's caused for so long. "They are her own blood! How could she be so cruel as to curse them and kill them?"

"Oh, but they aren't," he said as he pulled a couple of butterfly bandages from their packages.

"Wh—what?" I stuttered, looking at him with all the confusion I felt. "They aren't what?"

"They aren't her blood, dear." He pinched my skin together and began placing the first bandage. "Remember, I told you that my family has been the Campbell's physicians for centuries?"

I began to nod until I remembered to hold still for him and instead whispered, "Uh huh."

"Well, we have all kept records of our patients. Usually, those records are discarded after some time passes, usually after death. But sometimes, a case or patient is interesting enough to keep the records. Elspeth Campbell, obviously, was an... interesting character. When I was a young lad, I used to read the old files and came across hers once." He placed a second bandage and reached for a third, holding it up. "This may overdo it, but I want to make sure that it holds tight so you can heal well. You shouldn't have a scar, but we'll put some ointment on it, and as long as you leave it alone, it should heal quickly without leaving one behind."

I quickly agreed, hoping that he would get back to Elspeth's file, wanting to prompt him to continue but fighting not to be rude.

Finally, Dr. Ewen pulled his gloves off and smiled at me. "My grandfather was there when she gave birth to a stillborn little boy."

My breath caught in my lungs, and a shiver went down my spine. He nodded at my reaction.

"From the way the file reads, this young woman was unhappy, depressed to have been forced to marry. But when she found out she was with child, her demeanor began to lighten. She still hated her circumstances, but she wanted that child. When he was born, already deceased, something broke inside her. She refused to let anyone take the child away from her and held him to her breast for three days. Until her husband finally went to her and forced the child away. From then on, she was a hateful, spiteful woman."

"But she had another son..." I trailed off as the doctor shook his head.

"No, dear. She didn't. During the birth, she had complications. Refusing treatment for those days that she mourned caused her to have an infection that rendered her barren. The boy that was the next Campbell heir was not from Elspeth. Back in those days, an heir was necessary to continue a family line and lay claim to the family land. The lord would find a woman to bear him a son and expect his wife to raise him as her own."

"Oh no," I whispered in horror. A crazed and angry Elspeth would never tolerate such a thing. If she had the knowledge to curse her husband and his entire line for doing that to her, she would.

"Yes," he sat back and sighed, looking up at my newly bandaged cut. "I don't know why she would have attacked you, though. Generally speaking, it's usually the family or servants that have worked at the Manor for a long period of time that she seems to feel threatened by."

Yes, that was the million-dollar question. Why me? What threat was I to her? Why did the old woman that the librarian take me to tell me she had been expecting me?

The doctor stood up, and I quickly followed suit. "If you need any more assistance, don't hesitate to see me, though I would offer up my unsolicited advice." He stared down at me, his green eyes concerned and his wrinkled face the most serious I had seen it. "You aren't safe. She is escalating her violence. She killed Ian Campbell before he could even produce an heir, and now she's set her sights on you. You can't win against a ghost, dear. You should leave. Go back to America and forget you ever stepped into Moreland Manor."

With those parting words, he tipped his chin at me and then walked out the door, leaving it open for me. I saw his retreating back heading further down the hall, away from the exit sign. I sighed and walked back toward the front, and waited for the receptionist to end the phone call she was on. Once she finally turned to me with a smile, I tentatively smiled back.

"I, uh, wanted to find out how I pay for my service?" I asked and waved to the bandage on my head. She smiled wider as she explained the short version of how the healthcare system worked in Scotland.

My mind was swirling with all I had learned in the last half-hour. I wanted to feel sorry for Elspeth. Part of me ached for that young woman who hadn't been given a choice and for all that she lost. But the largest part was angry at her. She had the right to feel upset that she had no say in her life. She also had a right to grieve the loss of her only child. What she didn't have the right to do was torment an entire family line. Her vengeance was misplaced.

I slipped back into my seat and turned to Doogal with a grateful smile. His eyes went straight to the white bandage that stood out starkly against my dark hair. "Thank you for the ride and for waiting for me."

He grunted and then turned the key in the ignition. As we pulled away from the curb and slowly made our way down the cobblestone street, I couldn't stop fidgeting. There was a heaviness to the atmosphere in the car, so I wasn't surprised when he began speaking low and serious. Since Doogal had always been jovial and had never pried into personal matters, even after seeing me distraught more than once, it was a sharp contrast to hear him so solemn.

"Miss Lacey," he started out, his voice quiet but his tone determined. "Are ye sure that you should stay here?"

I turned in my seat just a bit so I could face him better. It was easy to notice with his complexion how very uncomfortable he was with the discussion already, and it had barely gotten started. It was endearing.

"Why do you ask?" I couldn't give away too much if he hadn't figured out my secret yet. I wasn't purposely trying to keep my activities from everyone, but I had a feeling that hiding from everyone was practically impossible. But even if they did know I was essentially ghost hunting, or at least hunting her past so I could save what was left of a family, I couldn't reveal my biggest secret. Ian didn't want to hurt his sister or niece by letting them know he was still around. I had to respect that.

His short glare shot my way before focusing back on the road and spoke loud and clear about how much he didn't appreciate my deflection. "You have been hurt since you've been here, and it's been such a short time. Most don't make it past physical altercations." He paused and scratched at his reddish-gray stubble filling the lines of his cheek. "I can drive you back to the airport on Monday if you get yerself packed up tomorrow."

I was already shaking my head. I was in much too deep. There was no backing away. I was the only one that could put a stop to everything.

"I appreciate it, Doogal. I do. But I need to be here."

He huffed out a disgruntled sigh, but he wasn't the type of person to push. He just nodded once. I thought the discussion was over, but when he pulled up to the doors of the Manor just as the sun was beginning to set, bathing the front of the structure in dark shadows, he decided he had more to say. I got out of the car and was walking up the steps when he hurried past me. He blocked my entry into the house with his hand on the doorknob.

"If you need help, you ask. Do ye hear me, Miss Lacey?" I nodded, eyes wide as he touched his fingers to the brim of his hat and then swung the heavy wooden door open to reveal the darkness of the great hall. "It's about time someone put that witch in 'er place."

And then he was gone, leaving me alone to stare up at the second floor, where a ghostly figure stood waiting for me at the top of the stairs.

Sixteen

I held Ian's gaze as I ascended the stairs. His eyes tracked my progress as I drew closer. They moved from my face slightly to catch on the white bandage taped over my temple. The look of concern as he looked at my injury brought warmth to fill me.

"It's okay," I whispered as I reached the top stair and stood still, not moving that final step to the landing. I reached up and gently prodded the small cut. "It really wasn't that bad. It didn't even need a stitch. I'm not supposed to get it wet, though. I guess the shower I wanted will have to wait."

He stretched out a hand, not grabbing me but allowing me the choice to take it. I didn't hesitate to reach for it, needing the connection more than I needed my next breath. The gentle warmth that he radiated was just another juxtaposition to the almost transparentness of his form.

Once my hand was in his, he gently pulled me forward until I had to take that last step up to reach his body. He kept pulling until my body was flush with his, and he looked back to the bandage. He raised his free hand to gently touch where I had just a moment ago, so lightly I could barely feel it.

"*I don't like that she hurt you,*" his gruff tone warmed me further. Knowing that he was so concerned for me made the feelings that had already been blooming inside me spread and become stronger than was probably smart. I was past the point of being smart, though, when it came to this man. I was at the point where it didn't matter anymore that he wasn't safe to have feelings for.

I blinked back the moisture that unexpectedly filled my eyes, making his translucent form waver. The harsh look on his face softened as he saw the emotion dancing in my eyes and slid his fingers from the bandage and down my cheek, caressing me there. In his gaze, I could see something that gave me hope, and my breath caught. I didn't want to analyze what I was seeing too deeply, but it was there, no matter how much I tried to pretend it wasn't.

Quickly, before I could protest, his strong arms swept me up to cradle my body against his chest. His face went into my hair for the briefest of seconds before he said with a thick voice, *"If you want a shower, then that's what you are going to have."*

He turned and began walking, carrying me as if I didn't weigh any more than a child. Once we reached my room, the door standing open, he walked through and gently kicked it until it snicked shut quietly. Still holding me close, he reached out with a hand and turned the lock.

He continued to carry me until we reached the bathroom and set me down on the counter. Turning to start the shower, I was able to study his body encased in his dark jeans and black shirt. He was so broad, his shoulders and arms filling out the sleeves in a way that made me want to sigh in appreciation of the glorious male form in front of me. I hardly had a glimpse of how well his bottom filled his jeans before he turned back to me, catching me in the act of ogling him.

He gave me a devilish grin and stepped into me, nudging my knees apart to get as close as possible. *"Your shower awaits, m'lady."*

I couldn't help the giggle at his deepened accent. Why the brogue sent tingles through me, I didn't know, but I wasn't going to fight it. I wasn't going to fight anything anymore.

He brought his hands to my knees and leisurely slid them up my thighs to the bottom of my shirt. Slowly, so slowly, he gave me enough time to voice a protest that would never come. He lifted my shirt up and carefully pulled it over my head, ever conscious of my bandage. Once the shirt was off, he stopped and stared at the satin baby blue bra I wore.

The heat that filled his eyes made me shift but, with him between my legs, I was unable to squeeze my legs together as my body wanted to do. His head bent forward, and he placed his lips on mine, not taking, just giving. That warmth that had started while we were by the stairs began spreading further, as my skin prickled with awareness of his desire. I pressed my chest into his as he moved his mouth over mine, wanting to be as close to him as I could. Then he suddenly stepped back.

I felt cool air cover me and looked down to see his hands pulling the straps of my bra over my arms. The sneaky devil had unhooked my bra while distracting me with his lips.

His wicked grin was too much to allow me to be irritated by his underhandedness. He tossed the lace to the side and reached for the button of my jeans next. Before I could attempt to protest, if I even wanted to, his mouth was on mine again. This time, he pressed more firmly and licked the seam of my lips until I opened them with a gasp.

I vaguely felt the button give and the zipper slide down. I was so entranced by the feel of his tongue sweeping over mine, I whimpered when he pulled away. Leaning forward to try to follow him, he took advantage of my raised chin and bent his head to nibble on my neck instead of reaching for my lips. I couldn't help the moan of frustration that instantly morphed into raw hunger as his lips and tongue played over the sensitive skin there.

My heart was beating rapidly as he seduced me with his mouth and hands that had started sliding from my loosened waistband up my ribcage to glide to my breasts. His rough stubble gently scraped over the sensitive skin of my neck as his thumbs swept over my tightened nipples. The dual sensations had me moaning, needing something more.

His head lowered further, his tongue gliding over my skin until I felt it there, covering a nipple that one of his hands held up for him in offering. A soft draw of my nipple into his mouth made an embarrassingly loud moan leave me. His chuckle vibrated against my chest until he drew away completely.

I had to fight myself from reaching out to grab him by the back of his head and force him to treat my other breast with the same attention. But before I could think twice, he had me on my feet and my jeans sliding down over my hips and down to my knees.

"*Out*," he commanded. I was helpless to do anything other than obey. He held me steady as I fought with kicking off my shoes in order to get the pants off completely. Once I was finally free, the hands that were on my hips moved again, this time to slide my panties down to meet the jeans on the floor.

Embarrassment started to fill me at being completely exposed, even though he had already seen me just like this before when he grabbed my waist and plopped me back down on my perch on the sink. The embarrassment quickly fled when I saw his hands go to his own shirt next.

"*I don't know how this is going to work,*" he commented as he pulled the shirt over his head, doing that maneuver that only men seemed capable of, pulling from behind his head to whip his shirt off. We both stared at it as he held a hand out and then finally let it drop.

I don't know what we had both expected to happen, but seeing the shirt lay there on the white tile, still mostly translucent, wasn't quite it. It seemed strange seeing it laying there. A ghost shirt was laying on my bathroom floor. It was so absurd that a giggle bubbled out of my throat. His head whipped up from where he had been staring at it with a perplexed look and pinned on me as I raised my hands to my mouth, trying to stifle the laugh. He just grinned and shook his head before reaching down to pop the button on his own jeans, immediately making my giggles cut off and my breath catch.

His eyes didn't leave mine as he drew his zipper down and began to tug the pants down over his muscular thighs. I didn't know how I hadn't noticed how tight they were, how snugly they hugged those thick thighs, but I was noticing now. He toed his shoes off and stepped out of the denim, leaving him wearing nothing but black boxer briefs that concealed nothing.

It was the first time I was in the same room as an almost naked man, and it was everything I had hoped it would be. My fantasies alone at night were nothing compared to the man that was standing in front of me. His cock was perfectly outlined under the cotton that was straining with the effort to hold it in place. It wasn't winning the battle.

As I stared, it jumped, making me startle and burst out with another giggle. He sighed heavily and leaned into me to place a kiss on the edge of my mouth.

"What am I going to do with you, darling?"

While I tried to hold in my giggles that were boarding on hysterical with my nervousness, he shucked off his underwear and scooped me back into his arms. I was disappointed that I hadn't had a chance to see what was pressed against my butt. I didn't have long to be disappointed, though.

He set me on my feet, far enough out of the spray to ensure my hair and, thus, my bandage would remain dry. As he reached for a washcloth, I finally had a chance to see his cock in all its glory. All it did was make me want to get closer. It was large. Large enough to cause a bit of trepidation to run through me, but I pushed it back with a firm shove. I was a woman, and I wanted to act like one. An inexperienced one, perhaps, but what I lacked in experience, I made up for with my eagerness.

He brought the soapy cloth to my chest and slowly, methodically, began to wash every inch of my skin. He started with my torso and didn't stop until he was on his knees in front of me, running the cloth over my calves and down to my feet.

Once he was satisfied that he had cleaned every bit that could get wet without consequence, he tossed the cloth to the side and reached for my hips, pulling me the step needed to come up to him from where he was on his knees. He held me there for a moment, looking up at me, his mossy green eyes not muted by his lack of solidity. Then, finally, he broke eye contact.

A gasp left me the moment his tongue met my center. There was nothing soft about the pressure against my clit. No, it was firm and enough to make me tremble. I desperately reached for his head, needing an anchor as he spread my legs further to allow him to have more access to my willing body.

"Fuck!" His growl against my pussy had more wetness rushing from me.

"Ian!" My hands clenched into fists, taking his length of hair into my hands tightly, but he didn't seem to notice or care as he pressed in closer.

He suddenly shifted, and I felt myself being moved until my back hit the cold tile wall, and one thigh was lifted over his broad shoulder. My hands never left his gorgeous hair as I screamed up into the shower ceiling, my head going back to thump against the wall. His tongue filling me was more than I could take. As his thumb pressed against my throbbing clit and he thrust his tongue inside of me, I shattered into a million pieces.

He never allowed me to return to earth. Before I could catch my breath, he was snarling into my pussy, demanding, *"More!"* I was helpless to resist his demand. I didn't have a chance. Between his tongue, his teeth, and his fingers all working in tandem, he had me fly apart again until I was leaning over his back, panting, my screams fading into the tiled walls.

Seventeen

I was still breathing heavily, waiting for my heart to stop racing, and trembling with aftershocks when Ian wrapped me in a towel and carried me into the bedroom. All I could do was grip onto his wide shoulders and nuzzle into his neck.

I had never felt so calm despite my fast beating heart. I felt like I was floating, and it wasn't just because I was being carried in his strong arms.

"Are you still with me, darling?" His breath fanned over my cheek and he placed a kiss there.

My breathy, "Uh huh," seemed to be what he needed to hear, because he lay me down on the soft bedding and swept my hair back from my face. I half expected him to climb over me and finish what he'd started, but he just leaned over me, stroking my hair and my cheek. The look in his eyes as I stared up at him had me swallowing hard. It wasn't the look of lust. He looked like a man that *felt*. The heat that had been building inside of me since I had come home began to blaze into an inferno.

"Are you ready for me, mo ghràidh?" I reached up with trembling fingers and brushed the tips lightly over his brows, his cheeks, and down to his lips, reveling in the way that warm look he was watching me with

softened even more. His green eyes were radiating something that his lips weren't saying. Something I was still a little scared to hear.

"Yes," I breathed out, fully aware that this was it, the moment I lost my heart completely.

His beautiful lips turned up in the corners and he finally lifted himself up and over me until his body completely covered me from head to toe. I had never felt warmer or safer. I never wanted to lose this feeling.

His lips came to mine and slowly coaxed my pleasure back to life. As he teased my lips, his hands began to wander, sliding over my breasts. Everything he did was soft and gentle. Even as he took his time, my breathing picked up. I was beginning to writhe in anticipation under his careful ministrations.

"Ian," I whispered, trying to tell him without speaking the words that I needed him.

"Yes, my darling?" he said between kisses that he had begun to trail over my collarbone.

"You're teasing me." Was that my voice? Breathy and sultry? I had never heard myself that way before. I slid one of my hands from his shoulder and up into his hair, threading through the strands. Both hands gripped tight, one hand digging nails into his shoulder and the other holding tight, once again, to his thick hair when his mouth found my breast. The sensation was exquisite. Little bolts of electricity shot through me, reaching every part of my body, but settled into one place. My core was throbbing, waiting for what only he could give me. "Please!" I called up to the canopy.

"Soon," he whispered as he left me panting, leaving the first breast with a gentle lick and swiped that wicked tongue over to the other, lonely one. He paid that one as much thorough attention as the first. My back bowed when he sucked deeply, bringing a gasp and then a long, low groan when he released his lips to gently lick across the sensitive peak.

Everything he was doing was designed to drive me mad with want. I couldn't have been more ready for him. After what he had done in the shower and then his current slow worship of my body, I was on the verge of screaming in frustration. And he had just gotten started.

Worship was exactly what he was doing. He was paying homage to my body. His hands slid and kneaded over my flesh everywhere he could easily reach. He ran his hands along my arms, down my sides, over my hips. Finally, finally, he reached down and firmly grasped one of my thighs and lifted it, bending my knee, giving himself the perfect place to rest his hips flush with mine.

He lifted his head with one last lick of my nipple and stared deeply into my eyes. No words were said between us, silently communicating with our eyes as he rotated his hips, sliding his cock over my mound. For several seconds all he did was watch me and slide himself softly against me. I felt the heat of his cock, so much warmer and firmer than I had felt him to be since we had first met. He slid over my clit, bathing himself in my wetness.

In a longer slide, he slipped down to notch the tip at my entrance. There, he paused and brought both of my hands from where I was gripping him and slid his hands up my arms to intertwine our fingers, gripping my hands tightly next to my head. With his elbows holding him up and staring right into my soul, he slowly slid forward.

The stretch was what I had expected, but it was so much more. I hadn't known how it would feel to have every nerve ending in my pussy being caressed by his cock as he slowly withdrew and pressed forward, making his cock slide deeper inside with every retreat and advance. The feeling of being filled, stretched, for the first time and the look in his eyes as he did so was too much to bear.

Overwhelmed, I closed my eyes and lifted my chin, trying to escape the connection that was too strong, too powerful.

"Mo ghràidh?" he called out to me softly, but with a firmness to his tone that I couldn't ignore. My eyes popped back open, and I lowered my chin so we were once again staring into each other's eyes. *"You stay. Right here with me. Understand?"*

As he slid in another inch, I nodded and swallowed as a tear slid from my eye, soaking into the bandage at my temple. He groaned and dipped his head, kissing me deeply as he finally reached the end of me. We were pressed so tightly together, not even air was welcome between us.

When he finally broke our kiss, he lifted his head and with a heated look, he said, *"Now, I will love you."*

My breath caught at his words, my brain trying to translate them into something other than sex. Before I could delve too deep into their meaning, he let go of my hands, slid one arm under mine to wrap up to hold firmly onto my shoulder. The other went back down to my thigh that he had lifted earlier and gripped it firmly, pressing it against his ribcage.

His thrusts that had been agonizingly slow changed. They were still slow, though they had increased in pace, but they were stronger. Each thrust pressed deep, as if he couldn't bear to part from me for long. Over and over, those sensations that had tingled and sparked electric strikes low in my belly became stronger. By the time he had made several strokes, I was crying out loud, unable to hold in my pleasure any longer.

He held my eyes with every slide and thrust, low grunts coming from his throat. Together, we were making a special kind of music, one I wanted to experience again and again for the rest of my life.

His strokes became less smooth, his grunts louder as he bottomed out inside of me harder. His jaw was tight and his muscles tense. I hadn't even noticed I had placed my hands back on his body, gripping him tight until I realized that I was digging my fingernails into his back. By then, I couldn't bring myself to care or to let go.

The pressure finally built to a crescendo that I was helpless to do anything but fall over. With a scream, I shut my eyes and exploded into a million pieces, not knowing if I would ever come back together, but knowing I would never be the same again.

Through the haze of my own release, I could feel Ian shove his face into my neck, his hand on my thigh so tight it was likely to leave bruises, and his grip on my shoulder crushing our bodies together. His deep, guttural grunt into my skin had a whimper leaving me. It wasn't because of how hard and close he was holding me, or how deep he was pressed into me, it was knowing that I had brought him that much pleasure.

As we lay there, both of our hands slowly let go of the harsh holds we had on each other. I felt him gently rub the flesh that he had been gripping on my thigh and I did the same on the crescent nail marks I had left on his back. Neither one of us made an attempt to part yet, though.

It was several long moments as we breathed each other in before he lifted his head and glanced down into my eyes. He ran his gaze over my face as if he were looking for any sign of discomfort, but he would find nothing but complete and total satisfaction and bliss.

He lowered his mouth to mine, and just like how he had started, he gently kissed me, making me want to weep at the sweetness. When he lifted his mouth from mine, he kissed my cheek, then both of my eyes, before placing a soft kiss on the tip of my nose. He slowly pulled out of me, leaving me feeling empty.

"I will be right back, darling," he spoke softly as he backed away and climbed off the bed. *"Don't move."*

I turned on my side and watched him pad into the bathroom, admiring the movement of muscles rippling under his skin with every step. I listened as the water turned on and off again before he reappeared, coming right back to my side. I blinked up at him, holding a washcloth, and then flushed when I realized what the cloth was for. I tried to reach out for it, but he chuckled.

"No, mo ghràidh, *it is my pleasure to clean you."* Then he gently nudged my legs apart and swiped the cloth gently over my center, cleaning me of both of our releases. I had a thought of what it meant that he would be able to release at all in his... condition. I supposed ghosts would still be able to? It was highly doubtful that there would be any worry of pregnancy from a ghost, though. That would take this entire situation into a realm beyond weird.

"Thank you." My whisper was so quiet he likely could barely hear me at all, but he still smiled at me and leaned down for another light kiss.

"As I said, it is my pleasure." Then he was gone again, walking back silently into the bathroom to drop the cloth into the sink. He returned after turning off the light and then slid under the covers with me.

His arms went around me and I snuggled into the crook of his arm. I breathed deeply to smell him until I realized I couldn't. There was no scent to him at all, and if I didn't feel the pressure of his arms and the very slight warmth of his skin, I wouldn't know he was there at all.

As I began to fall asleep to the feel of him brushing a kiss over the top of my head, a deep sadness washed over me. He was only half with me. I would never have more than what I had right now with him. Even if I was never able to break the curse and release all the souls of the ghosts trapped in the Manor, Ian and I could never have a true relationship. He wasn't *real*. We couldn't get married. Never have children.

It was with those depressing thoughts as I was drifting off to sleep that I felt my body drop against the bed. I sat up quickly and ran my hands over the sheets where he had just been moments before. A sob tore from my throat and I wrapped my hands around my knees, burying my head into them.

Ian was gone.

Eighteen

I woke with the sun, my hand stretched out, reaching for a body that wasn't there. It was a harsh reminder of the night before. I groaned, clenching my hand into a fist and rolled onto my back and just stared up into the canopy. I couldn't help but think of our night as I lay there in the weak morning light.

Everything about the experience was beautiful and perfect. Everything except the end, when he disappeared. I squeezed my legs together while I replayed what he had done to me and felt the slight discomfort. Somehow, that ache just made me miss him more.

I rolled back to my side, facing where he had been laying last night. The indentation in the pillow was a stark reminder that he was never guaranteed to be around. I wish I knew why he disappeared and where he went. Considering he had no idea either, I supposed I would never know.

With a sigh, I sat up and swung my legs over the side of the bed and sat there facing the window. The drapes were partially open, explaining why the room was as bright as it was. The sun hadn't been up for long, but I could already see that it was likely to be another pleasant day. That was good, since I still needed to head over to the local cemetery today. I couldn't put it off much longer.

I thought of the witch and exploring her room yesterday and shuddered, wrapping my arms around my body at the sudden chill I felt deep in my bones. I hoped I would never experience anything so awful again in my life. Honestly, I was surprised that I didn't have nightmares. Though that was probably because after Ian disappeared I was drowning in a grief so strong I ended up crying myself into an exhausted heap.

I was debating on trying to lay back down for more rest and getting up to sneak in some coffee when there was a soft tapping on my bedroom door. I twisted around from my position on the bed so I could stare at the door in horror, as if the witch were there waiting to jump out and grab me.

"Lacey? It's Isla. Can we talk?"

Pressing a hand to my chest to calm my racing heart, I blew out a harsh breath and mentally scolded myself. The witch would never knock—locked doors meant nothing to her. If she wanted to attack me, she could easily do so. Which made me wonder why I hadn't heard or seen her since yesterday. Perhaps she expended too much energy and had to wait before she could manifest again. It would explain a lot. It would also explain why Ian had disappeared, too.

"One minute!" I called out. I jumped up and quickly went to the wardrobe to pull out a shirt and sweatpants. A ball of dread filled the pit of my stomach, the same as it used to do when my parents would call me to the living room when I was a kid to lecture me from some mischief I had gotten up to. I had been expecting this talk, I just hoped it wouldn't be unpleasant.

I dragged my feet as I walked over to the door, trying to delay the inevitable. I brushed my disheveled hair back and squared my shoulders, placing a smile on my face that I hoped didn't look too fake. Finally, I twisted the lock that Ian had put in place and grabbed the knob, swinging the door open wide.

I don't know what she saw when she looked at me, but her eyebrows went clear to her hairline. She held out one of the two cups she was holding and I could smell coffee wafting from it. I immediately brought it to my mouth with a groan and blew on it, ready to devour it.

"Um," she began, and waved a hand inside the room. "Do you mind if we have a chat?"

I looked back at the room with the messy bed covers and the one chair in the corner. My cheeks grew warm at what I did there last night with her brother. I cleared my throat and stepped back. "Yes, of course."

I stood back to allow her entrance and watched as Isla tried to look around inconspicuously, but I could imagine she was trying to see if I were hiding a man in my room. She was nothing but grace personified as she took a seat in the chair and crossed her legs, holding her teacup daintily in one hand.

"I appreciate you letting me talk to you privately this morning. I didn't want our conversation to reach little ears."

"I understand," I murmured as I took a perch on the end of the bed and crossed my legs in front of me. I brought my cup close to my face and fantasized about disappearing inside the liquid to avoid what was likely to be an awkward conversation.

She cleared her throat, making me bring my eyes back to her. "Yes, so, I wanted to ask how your... exploring went yesterday?"

I swallowed thickly. Oh shit. What did I say? *Stick to the basics.* "I, ah, found the room I was looking for. It wasn't quite what I expected." It wasn't exactly a lie.

"Oh?"

Damn, she wasn't going to give me an inch. I fidgeted and took another quick sip of coffee. "Yes. It looks like it hasn't been touched since she lived in it."

She grimaced. "I could imagine. She has always been a spectre in this family. No one ever liked to talk of her. Which is understandable, I suppose. As children, Ian and I were warned to stay away. No one talked about her much. There was only one time that my grandmother told me the story that I had told you." Pausing to take a long sip of her tea, she finally spoke again. "So, you didn't find anything in there?"

I stared at her and wondered what she was fishing for. I just shook my head, not daring to speak. She nodded, then rested her cup on the arm of the chair, her hand holding it steady.

"I know what you are trying to do, Lacey." Her tone was matter of fact and she stared at me, knowingly.

"You," I cleared my throat and started again. "You do?"

She sighed and looked over to the window where the light had gotten brighter as we sat there. "Honestly, I wish I could do what you are doing, but I have my little girl to think about." She looked back at me. "Others have tried to figure out how to stop her."

That surprised me. I was under the impression that the only one that had given any energy to finding out how to break the curse was the old woman from the village. "What did they find out?"

She shook her head sadly. "Nothing. There have been séances, priests, people that have come in with incense or sage trying to cleanse the Manor. Nothing helped."

That sounded... limited. From all that I have learned so far, Elspeth was too strong. She had too much of a hold on the place to just vanish with some chant or herbs wafting through the halls.

"A priest came?"

"Oh, yes. I was probably ten years old. My mother called in favors until the church agreed to bring in someone that was supposedly an expert in exorcisms. He walked in the door, stood there for about thirty seconds before he turned a ghostly shade of white, pardon the description, and promptly turned around to leave. He had refused to talk to anyone about what he had experienced in that short amount of time to just leave without trying." She shook her head in disgust. "Shameful."

That made me stop. I had so many thoughts running through my head; I needed a moment to recalibrate myself. I drained my coffee and set the cup next to my leg and folded my hands in my lap. "Do you hear her?"

Isla grimaced. "I have. I have heard screaming, and occasionally voices that are too difficult to understand clearly. It's not often, just a few times in my life." She cocked her head and looked at me in curiosity. "Is that what you hear?"

I didn't know what to say, so I decided to go with honesty... to a degree. "I've heard her screams, and I've heard the other ghosts whisper. But..." I cleared my throat. "I've seen her, too."

She gasped and almost choked on the sip she had been taking. "You've *seen* her?"

I nodded slowly. "I, um, I've had a couple of altercations with her."

Her eyes darted straight to the white bandage on my temple. "Is that where you got that? Did it happen in the room?"

I tentatively prodded the area and was relieved that it was just a dull ache when I touched it. "It did. It isn't bad, really. Ian sent me to the doctor just to make sure but…"

"*Ian!*" Isla shrieked, and it was the first time I had ever seen this elegant woman, a lady to her core, flustered. No, she wasn't flustered, she was freaked the hell out. "What? You *see* Ian? You *talk* to him?"

I flushed at the thought of what we did together. She didn't miss my reaction and shrieked again.

"Oh my god! You slept with him, didn't you? How is that even possible?"

Fuck. Fuckity fuck. I hadn't meant to say anything at all. He hadn't wanted to hurt his sister by letting her know he was still around and I had just ruined that.

"I'm so sorry, Isla." Ashamed, I let my head drop and unconsciously began tapping my wrist.

I didn't hear her get up, but I felt her kneel at the end of the bed and grab my hands in hers. Her grip was tight and when I chanced a look at her face, she looked ravaged, desperate.

"Is he okay? Is she torturing him?"

I shook my head and felt a tear slide down my cheek. "No. He isn't being tortured. He seems to be fine. He doesn't know where he goes when he's not here. But he is strong. Strong enough to keep her from hurting me. That's how I first saw him. She was…" I stopped and swallowed hard and glanced towards the open bathroom door where all I could see from my vantage point was most of the sink and a bit of the toilet.

I looked back at her and moved my hands so it was me squeezing her. "He's saved me. He's a hero. I don't know what I would have done if he hadn't come along. More than once."

"And you've fallen in love with him." It wasn't a question.

My body jerked, my instinct to deny it, to tell her it was nothing. But after last night, the way he held me, looked at me, made love to me so tenderly, I couldn't shame what we had done by dismissing it as nothing. I stifled a small sob and nodded my head. "I do. He's—he's wonderful. I hate that he can't be here. Like, for real. I hate knowing that he's dead because of her. I want to break her curse, vanquish her so she can't hurt anyone else. But..." I looked away as sorrow buried deep and let out another sob. "If I do—" I couldn't finish.

Isla let out a sound that was part distress and part sympathy as she quickly stood up and sat next to me and gathered me close. I wrapped my arms around her as tightly as she was holding me and I let it all out. I cried and shook as she sobbed out her heartbreak from losing her brother all over again.

Once we had cried ourselves out, Isla sat back and smoothed my damp hair from my cheeks. How she still looked so beautiful after a crying jag like that, I would never know.

"Oh, sweetie. I'm so sorry. If there were anything I could do to make this better, I would." She glanced at my bandage again and shook her head. Are you sure this is the path you want to take? If the witch has hurt you once, she can do it again."

I looked at her, eye to eye, and told her my truth. "If I don't end her and send her away for good, it could be Olivia that she hurts next."

Her face got hard and a fierceness I hadn't known she was capable of came over her. "Then I hope you destroy her and send her to hell."

Nineteen

I wasn't sure why it seemed like I was preparing to head into battle, but that's exactly how I felt as I pulled on my boots, slipping them over my favorite pair of jeans to rest against my calves. I stood up and smoothed down my long-sleeved cotton shirt before heading into the bathroom to pull my hair back into a ponytail.

As I stared into the mirror, I could see the trepidation I was feeling clearly written all over my face. I took in a long breath before letting it out slowly, glancing over to look at the makeup bag I rarely used, and withdrew a tube of mascara. I carefully swiped some on, trying to be careful not to smear it all over my eyelid, and cursed when I still managed to get a smudge above my left eye. I had little experience with makeup, only using it on rare occasions, so my application method could probably use some work.

With a sigh, I pulled out a cotton swab and lightly wet it in order to scrub the smudge off my eyelid. Once I was satisfied I didn't look like a three-year-old playing with mommy's make-up, I swiped on some clear lip gloss and called it good. My armor was in place, such as it was. If I did indeed need to go into battle today, at least I would look nice.

After zipping up and shoving the bag into one of the bathroom drawers, I flipped off the light and grabbed the light jacket that I had left lying on the end of the bed. I knew already that the sun was deceiving. The weather in Scotland was going to be chilly, and I didn't want to be caught freezing my ass off while hunting graves.

Finally ready to go, I quietly shut my bedroom door behind me and made my way down the corridor. Isla was going to take Olivia to the same library I had been in the other day for storytime and to pick out some books. I bit my lip, thinking about the angry librarian, and hoped she wouldn't think Isla was involved with what had happened. I'd hate for Moira to turn her anger towards her. Or worse, onto Olivia.

Instead of calling for a ride, I decided to walk to the cemetery. Isla had told me where to find it, as well as where her family plot was located. At least I would have a general idea of where to start looking instead of heading in the wrong direction.

The walk was pleasant and only took about thirty minutes. I had been wise to bring the jacket since there was a light breeze, making the sun's rays do little to burn away the chill in the air. As I came to the graveyard, my eyes widened at how large it was. I supposed that it was to be expected, really. That was the only place around that was available for the locals in the village to bury their loved ones for countless generations.

There was a small building ahead as I walked along the outside of the fence. I had been staring at all the graves as I passed, noticing the different types, heights, and ages, so engrossed in them that I hadn't noticed a small service being held further ahead. It was far enough away that I hoped they wouldn't notice me, and I was glad that it was in the opposite direction of where Isla had told me to go. The last thing I wanted to do was to intrude on their mourning.

I slipped through the open gate and turned back the way I had come, angling up toward the far corner. In the distance I could see larger stones, raised beds and a few mausoleums. For being the ruling family in the area, it made sense that they would have a large, private plot.

I carefully picked my way through the graves, relieved to spot a path that would help keep me from feeling guilty about walking over people's final resting places. It seemed so disrespectful.

I finally started seeing the last name Campbell and slowed down, beginning to carefully study each of the graves. There didn't seem to be a specific order to the stones. Some were as old as 1895, while I saw another that read 1943. Not every stone was a Campbell, I noticed. There were several dotted in with other last names that I guessed were close relatives that chose to be buried in the family plot. It was going to make my job of finding Elspeth Campbell that much more difficult.

I walked around a small mausoleum when a sight had me stopping in my tracks and my breath caught. My nose immediately began to burn, and I took a shuddering breath. Just ahead of me was a freshly turned grave, barely settled, with no grass growing over it yet.

I slowly walked forward and once I got within a step of the mounded dirt, I stopped and stared. Then I couldn't stop myself as I stumbled forward and gripped onto the headstone. I had to breathe hard to stop myself from sobbing.

"Ian." God. *God.* I didn't know why it hadn't occurred to me that I would find his grave here. Why hadn't it occurred to me? "Oh, Ian." I stifled a sob, squeezing my eyes shut against the pain that was piercing my heart. My hands were gripping the headstone so hard that my nails scraped against the surface.

In a few short moments, every single thing that I would never have a chance to experience with this man flooded my mind. Our wedding, our babies, holding each other's hands as we drove down the road, laughing about some inane story. Sitting together on our couch as we watched a movie while sharing a bowl of popcorn. Waking up next to each other just to smile at one another, knowing how, after so many years together, we were still so in love.

I thought of our babies growing and getting married. Of Ian dancing with our daughters on their wedding day and later, me holding my newborn grandbabies.

It was gone. All of it. I would never get that chance. Never have that life with the man I had fallen for so quickly and so completely. I couldn't deny the look in his eyes last night as he took me. He felt just as deeply for me as I did for him.

I looked up with dry, scratchy eyes. She did this. She had torn apart families for generations. For nearly two entire centuries, she had terrorized the people of the Manor, and *murdered* innocent people because *she* was unhappy with the hand life had dealt her. And I would be the hand that would end her reign of torment.

With hardened eyes and a fresh resolve, I bent down to the grass to pluck a tiny flower growing wild. I placed it on Ian's headstone, then with a last brush of fingertips over the freshly carved letters that spelled his name, I straightened my shoulders and began to look again. I would look until I found her.

Row after row I searched, not skipping a single plot. I even doubled back, so I would be sure to not miss a name. At the mausoleums, I scanned the plaques, finding Conal and Colleen Campbell in one, and smiled softly, sniffling again at the sudden emotion that came over me. Colleen and Conal were resting together forever. Just as they should. Though it was still much too soon, as I noticed the dates under their names. Colleen went to live on for another forty years, living into her seventies. Given her lack of name change, I assumed she had never remarried. It was heartbreaking.

"Don't worry, Colleen. I'll make sure she pays," I whispered, and gently smoothed my fingers over the plaque.

I turned to keep going, ready to continue my search, when I was brought up short. A man in a long black robe and a white collar had his hands folded in front of him as he slowly but steadily made his way up the path.

I looked behind him to where the service had been taking place and noticed the last line of cars leaving. Looking back at him, I realized he must have been conducting the service and seen me. Likely wondering what a stranger was doing wandering the graveyard. But, weren't graveyards open to the public so people could pay their respects? Maybe it was a small town thing.

His eyes were warm and his smile genuine as he finally made it to me and held out his hand. I hesitantly took it and gave him a small smile back.

"Hello, I don't believe I have seen you around here before?"

His statement was definitely a question, and he waited expectantly for my answer, not letting go of my hand as he studied my face. His hand was small and smooth, matching the rest of his stature. He was hardly taller than me and his head was as smooth as a baby's bottom.

"Uh, hi. I'm visiting," I hedged, not really sure what I should tell him. I would be committing a crime soon and the last thing I needed was for him to put two and two together, coming up with me as the culprit to grave desecration and being absolutely right.

He finally released my hand, and I stuffed it into my pocket, hoping to avoid touching him again. I hated being touched by strangers. It was part of the whole anxiety thing. My nerves were already on edge, and the way he was studying me wasn't helping anything.

"Ah, American, I hear." He tilted his head, even more intrigued. I just nodded once.

"Yes. That's right."

"On holiday, then?"

"I, uh, yes."

"Do you enjoy looking at graves? Is it the headstones that you like reading, or do you have a distant relative you are looking to find?" His interrogation was getting me flustered and I could feel the heat rising up my neck with every minute that passed, his little brown eyes staring so hard at me.

"I'm looking for a grave, actually," I finally answered, unable to come up with any plausible excuses at the spur of the moment as my nervousness continued to build.

His eyes lit up, and he rubbed his hands together. "Ah, lovely. Perhaps I can help you. This is a relative?"

"Er, no. Not exactly." I spun around to face the rest of the Campbell plot and wished for a miracle, for anything that would help me get this over with and away from the inquisitive little priest. Unfortunately, no neon sign began pointing and blinking saying 'here she is!'.

I heard him step forward until he was standing right next to me. It took everything I had inside me to not shrink away from him. He was standing so close our shoulders were nearly touching and I could feel his body heat through my jacket. It was too close for comfort. Too close to my personal boundaries. I was going to have an anxiety attack if I couldn't get away from him soon.

"Well, dear. Tell me who you are looking for. It's part of my duties, after all. I know most of these graves. And if there happens to be one that I don't know, I can easily find out."

My shoulders drooped in defeat. I couldn't see a way to put him off any longer. "I'm looking for Elspeth Campbell," I said quietly. I hadn't expected the sharp intake of breath, though I probably should have. She was a legend around here, after all. What I definitely hadn't expected was looking back at him to see his once kind and jovial eyes had turned hard as stone, with rage simmering within them.

His jaw was hard, and I couldn't help but notice that his hands were no longer folded gently in front of him, but clenched into fists at his sides.

I stumbled back and had to reach out to steady myself on the side of the mausoleum that I was still next to. I glanced up at the plaque and moaned in my head as clarity flooded in. *Oh Colleen, why didn't I just say I had been looking for you?* It was a plausible excuse, completely acceptable. But I had to let my nerves get me so flustered I didn't think straight.

"*Heathen*!" He practically hissed the word out. "You devil worshiper! How *dare* you come on to this holy ground!" He stomped his foot as if to emphasize the ground below us.

"I—I..." I was shaking my head frantically. "I don't under—"

"Your kind is not welcome here and never will be. Just like her kind is not welcome here" His anger was rabid, and he was slowly advancing towards me. "Get it through your thick, heathen skulls! That witch, Elspeth Campbell, was not welcomed into this hallowed ground two hundred years ago, and *you* are not welcome here now!"

"I'm not! I swear!" I tried one last time, knowing it was futile.

"Get. Out!" He leaned into me, my back pressed against the stone wall, with nowhere else to go. I could smell his breath and feel the warmth as he shouted directly into my face. I grimaced as I felt his spittle hit me on the cheek and the chin. "Don't ever come back!"

I slid out from between the wall and his hateful body and immediately began running for the entrance. I swiped at my face with my sleeve, disgust roiling inside me at the thought of his saliva on my skin.

At least I had done what I had come here to do. Sort of. I didn't find Elspeth's grave. But I did find where she was not.

Twenty

After eating a light lunch of a sandwich and a glass of juice in the conservatory, I walked up the stairs to my bedroom. My mind was spinning, trying to think of all the options of where Elspeth's grave could be. But, truly, I hadn't the first clue.

I figured that once I got to my room and kicked off my boots, I would resort to Google. Maybe there would be some information on where people were buried when they weren't permitted inside of a cemetery. It wasn't something I had heard of before, but didn't surprise me. Minds were much more narrow two hundred years ago. Thinking of the priest's reaction earlier today, I was beginning to believe that they hadn't widened much since then, either.

I swung open my door and closed it behind me, when I felt a presence in the room. I slowly turned around, the onslaught of fear that usually accompanied the witch's appearance was absent, so I knew who it had to be. My belly was already filling up with butterflies before I even saw him.

He stood up from the chair and watched me watch him for a long moment. Finally, he broke the silence.

"Darling."

I wanted nothing more than to run and jump into his arms, but I was still so shaken by the confrontation with the priest. And I could still feel the coolness of the marble on my fingertips from where I had ran them over his carved name.

"Ian," I breathed, not daring to take my eyes off of him. Some part of me was so afraid that he would vanish again if I looked away for even a moment.

He held his hand out to me from across the room, a knowing glint in his eyes. There was an apology there, too. He didn't need to say it, I knew he wouldn't have left me on purpose.

"Come to me."

It wasn't a demand, nor was it a question. It was an unspoken plea. It was at that moment that I realized he needed me to accept him as he was. And I did.

I dropped my jacket on the floor at my feet and before it had even settled in place, I was running the way my instincts had urged me to when I first looked up to see him sitting all alone, waiting.

His arms were open before I even reached him and they caught me, wrapping around me tightly as I barreled into him. His mouth was on mine in the next breath. Together, we gave into what we wanted and needed most. Connection. With firm hands, he grabbed me under my bottom and lifted, urging me to wrap my legs around his hips. Then one of his hands slid up to cup the back of my head to guide our kiss.

He was ruthless as he took my mouth, our kiss brutal, but full of all the passion we felt. His broad chest vibrated with a growl as he sucked and nipped at my lips.

"Mine," he whispered between kisses, making my heart swell with his possessiveness.

"Yours," I agreed on a pant. "Please, Ian. I need you so much!" I suddenly felt desperate to have him own my body again. I needed to feel that closeness to erase the memory of seeing his grave. I needed to know he was real.

With another growl, he stalked over to the bed without taking his mouth from mine. Once we reached the side, he dropped me and I landed with a small squeal. I quickly brushed the hair from my face so I could see him again and caught the look in his eyes as he pulled his shirt over his head. My breath caught at the feral look on his face. He looked starved, and what he was about to devour was me.

The soft and gentle lover from the night before was gone. In its place was a man that wouldn't be denied. That couldn't be denied. It made things happen inside me that I was unprepared for. A burning began to grow inside my core as he reached for his jeans and quickly undid the button. My chest was heaving by the time he began to yank them down his hips, not sure I was prepared for what he was going to do next, but still eager for it.

As he stepped out of his jeans, his hands were on me and I found myself quickly divested of my clothing, not even seeing where they landed. In one blink to the next, his head was between my legs and my fingers were threaded through his hair. I tipped my head back to the canopy with my mouth open, gasping for breaths.

"Ian!" My moans and whimpers just seemed to spur him on further as he made me see stars.

Before I even had a chance to catch my breath, a high pitched wail left me, then he was face to face, staring into my eyes as he slid himself into me slowly, allowing me to adjust to his size.

"I don't like being away from you," he ground out between clenched teeth, closing his eyes as he relished in the bliss that visibly consumed him as he filled me completely. *"I don't know if you are in danger, if I need to protect you."* He pulled out, the end of him resting at my entrance. Then he plunged back in sharply, making me scream in surprise at the sharpness of the pleasure.

He did the same thing several times, withdrawing slowly, then spearing back into me with a hard thrust until our pelvises met together. Then, with each retreat and thrust he grunted. *"I. Can't. Protect. You. And. It's. Killing. Me."*

I wrapped my arms and legs around him and held him as tight as I could to me. I clenched onto his broad back, digging my fingertips into his muscles as they flexed with his movement. "Oh, Ian. I'm sorry!" I cried out with pleasure, but also with the pain in my heart from knowing he was scared for me.

He kissed me deeply, his movements speeding up, carrying both of us to the ultimate precipice. Together we gasped into each other's open mouths, not willing to part, not caring to breathe. My only need was him. His only need was me.

"*You're mine*, mo ghràidh. *You know that, don't you? I won't leave you. I swear I will find a way to stay with you. I swear it!*"

With a final thrust, he buried himself deeply and groaned into my neck. I screamed into the canopy as my body shook with pleasure. I hadn't realized that I was crying until I felt Ian lean back up and swipe at the tears soaking into my hair and bandage. I sniffled as I looked into his eyes.

"I—" I sniffled again and swallowed hard. Our time was fleeting. We had no time to play games or skirt around the truth. I didn't know how long it would take me to find the missing grave. It could be tomorrow if I were... lucky. Not that my heart felt lucky. No, it felt like it was breaking over and over again every time I thought of the future. He had made me a promise that I was certain would be impossible for him to keep. But I would keep his words with me until the day I died. With a deep breath, I pushed away the vulnerability that was crowding my lungs at the thought of rejection. Of being told it was too soon. This was my truth. I knew it to my soul. This was why I was brought here, clear across the globe, for him. Not just to fight a centuries old curse. Not just to protect a precious little girl from meeting the same fate her ancestors had. It was him. This man. This ghost.

"I love you, Ian." My words were hardly more than a whisper, a breath hanging in the still air between us. But he heard. His eyes went soft and one corner of his mouth tipped up.

"*Oh, my darling. I feel for you so deeply. From the moment I saw you in the bath, looking terrified and confused. You captured my heart. I may not be a man anymore, but my heart only beats for you. I swear,* mo ghràidh, *I swear that I will find a way for me to stay. I will fight the very gods if I need to.*"

I sobbed out a laugh and wrapped my arms around his neck. Did I believe that he would stay? Not really. But my heart soared with hope. I wouldn't live a normal life, but I would be happy every day of it. As long as I had him.

. . .

***

We lay together for hours, talking quietly, our fingers intertwined. My eyes often drifted there, taking in the differences. He was large, dwarfing my fingers, but that wasn't what had me fascinated. It was the way his flesh was translucent, insubstantial. It was strange, being able to see my own flesh through his.

He took me several more times that night, neither one of us resting. I felt like we were both trying to deny what the near future would bring. As if by avoiding sleep, we could avoid him disappearing. I knew we both feared that the next time would be the last.

Eventually, my eyes grew heavy, and I could hardly keep them open. I felt him kiss my eyelids as if in a fog. I heard his whispered promises of tomorrow, and even though my soul cried out, my body couldn't stop the descent into sleep.

I woke to a dim light as the sun tried to weakly cut through the morning fog. Alone. Before I could let myself break into the sorrow that was crowding my chest, making it difficult to breathe, I took a deep breath. I had a job to do. I had no time for self-pity.

I hugged the pillow his head had been resting on close to my chest and buried my face into, taking strength from him even though he wasn't there to provide it. I inhaled, hoping to catch even the slightest whiff of scent left behind, but again, there was nothing.

I drifted back into sleep as I held on to the pillow until I woke with a scream. My dream had been vague, difficult to understand as I had wandered through the empty halls of the Manor. Nothing was the same as it should be. It looked old, rundown. Resembling more a haunted house that had been abandoned for years than a beautiful stately Manor with gleaming tables and flowers in antique vases. I was wearing a diaphanous blue gown that clung to my chest and swept out around my bare feet. My hair loose and hanging in waves down my back.

As I wandered the halls, I began to grow more and more desperate. Something was hunting me. I knew I was looking for something. Someone. But I couldn't figure out who or what it was. I was calling out for someone, but in my dream state, I didn't know who.

I came to the stairs, my hand gliding over the banister as I began to descend, but stopped when I heard an eerie scream tear through the still, musty air. It raised goosebumps all over my body and my heart nearly stopped in my chest before galloping away quickly in my chest. I froze on the step, a few feet down from the top and, even though I wanted to run down them as fast as I could until I reached the safety of outside, I slowly turned to face what I could sense was behind me. Terror filled every inch of my being as I finally saw what was hunting me.

The black eyes of an older woman stared at me with disdain and unconcealed malevolence. She was dressed in all black from a period before my time, the collar buttoned up tightly to her neck stood at the top of the stairs.

"You!" she hissed. "You don't belong here!"

I backed down a step, trying to back away from her rage. "I—I don't…"

"You are never going to be the mistress here! I am! That won't be taken away from me!"

"I'm not! I swear!" I cried out, carefully taking another step, feeling for the marble of the staircase with my toes.

"He will make you the mistress! I won't allow it!"

As I shook my head wildly, she began to morph into something hideous. The black dress that had been pristine, though severe looking, frayed at the hem and cuffs, wrinkles developed before my eyes and it ripped, looking aged. Her hair turned gray in its bun and frizzed around her wrinkled face. Her teeth yellowed and cracked as her sneer turned from rage to completely evil.

"Leave! Leave and never return to this house!" She screamed and flew at me, not touching the marble. I stumbled back, terror clogging my throat. As I tried to scramble away from her, my feet lost purchase, slipping on the edge of the smooth stair and I fell.

I felt every hit to my body as I tumbled. As I lay broken at the bottom of the staircase, the witch hovered directly over my body, suspended in midair, hardly a breath away from me. She grinned as she watched me bleed onto the dirty, leaf strewn floor. And laughed. And then she disappeared.

Twenty-One

It was Monday morning again. That meant that I had responsibilities that didn't include hunting down a witch's unmarked grave.

I was sitting at the wooden table with Olivia, watching her count the apples on the sheet in front of her. But my mind kept drifting. The possibilities were endless. An unmarked grave of a person that may not actually be a witch, but certainly earned the title as a murderess, could be anywhere. What if she had been cremated? I didn't even know if they did that in the 1800s. Though I thought I remembered somewhere that they had, hadn't I?

But, of course, that couldn't be possible. If her bones had been destroyed by fire, there wouldn't be a tether holding her here. Since she haunted the Manor, did that mean she was buried nearby? Maybe on the grounds? That didn't seem right, either. I couldn't imagine Colleen, the last remaining adult, permitting her mother-in-law to be buried anywhere near.

"That's perfect, honey!" I praised Olivia as she smiled up at me with a toothy grin.

"I did good?"

"You did great! I'm so proud of you. Why don't we set this aside and you can work on your letters until Miss Chasity comes for you?"

She agreed readily, always eager to learn. We spent the next twenty minutes going over her letters, and I felt confident that she would be writing well by the end of winter. When Chasity came to collect her, I was torn. I didn't want to leave Olivia's side. The growing panic that she was going to be targeted by Elspeth, and the need to continue my research so I could end the threat once and for all, warred inside me.

I finally came to a decision I truly didn't want to make. I knew of only one person in this village that might have insight on where I could find the grave. I needed to go back to the library and try to convince Moira to let me talk to her grandmother again.

With my mind made up, I quickly gathered Olivia's papers and put them away neatly on the shelf, then pulled out my phone.

Doogal met me at the front door and, kind as ever, held my car door for me, waiting for me to get settled before shutting it firmly. We made small talk as we drove the short distance into the village. I had seen him glance at my temple, but I had removed the gauze. All that was left behind was the small strips that would remain until the stitches fell off. And, of course, bruising. But I was certain it didn't look too bad. It actually didn't hurt at all unless I pressed on it.

"I'm okay, I promise," I said in a quiet voice. "I appreciate you taking me to the doctor the other day. And today, of course. I was thinking that maybe I could get a bicycle, so I don't have to keep troubling you for rides."

He grunted and waved a hand dismissively in the air. "'Tis no trouble. But if ye want a bike, we can find ye one."

"That would be wonderful! Thank you!" I grinned at the side of his weathered face and saw his ear turn red with embarrassment at my happiness at his words.

"Ye be careful on these roads. And watch the skies. No cause to be stuck in a downpour if ye can help it."

"I will," I promised, as I nearly bounced in my seat with excitement. I hadn't ridden a bike in years, but I was sure the independence I'd gain from learning how again would be worth any tumbles I might take. They say you never forget how to ride and I hoped that was true.

We pulled up to the front of the library and I took a deep breath before climbing out of the car. I clasped my hands in front of me as they shook in trepidation. When we parted last, Moira had looked ready to murder me and I wasn't eager to face her again.

As I pulled the door open, I took several more calming breaths and tapped my forefinger against the wrist of my other hand, needing to ground myself. *It would be okay. Everything would be okay.*

Instead of walking straight to the round desk in the center of the room, I detoured down the first aisle of books and ran my finger over the spines. I was in the mystery section. I hadn't read any of the books I saw there, but I had heard of a few authors on the shelves. I turned the corner, planning on delaying the inevitable for as long as possible.

"What are you doing here?" A voice hissed at me, making me stop in my tracks.

Moira was standing right in front of me with her arms crossed. She didn't look nearly as angry as she had the last time we parted ways, but she definitely wasn't happy to see me.

I waved awkwardly. "Um, Moira, hi. Um, how is your grandmother?"

It was the wrong thing to say. Her eyes flashed and she pointed towards the exit. "Get out!" Her voice never raised, a true librarian to her core, but the inflection there told me she meant business.

I clasped my hands in front of me and raised them to my chin and gave her the biggest puppy eyes I could. It was a childish move, something I used to do when I was a little girl begging for something that my parents had already denied me. It had almost always worked then, and I had to fight dirty now.

"Please, Moira. I need help!"

Her eyes darted from my face, down to my hands, then back to my face several times before she huffed in disgust. Then she turned on her heel and began walking away. I watched her in dismay until she hissed out a quiet, "Come on, then!" without stopping.

I smiled and dropped my hands, hurrying after her. She led me to a door marked Employees Only and held the door open for me. I saw a small round table, a short refrigerator, and a counter with a coffeepot and electric teakettle sitting neatly there.

"Have a seat," she gestured to one of the chairs and pulled out one for herself, dropping into it heavily and crossing her arms. I slowly lowered myself into the chair she had indicated and waited for her to speak again. "What do you want, Lacey?"

I started to open my mouth when she interrupted. "You have five minutes. Make it count."

I nodded eagerly. "Your grandmother told me I need to find Elspeth's grave." I waited until she reluctantly nodded, her lips pressed into a thin line. "I searched the cemetery until a priest came along. When I asked him about it, he... he got super angry. He started yelling at me." I grimaced and stared down at the lacquered tabletop. "He called me a devil worshiper and told me never to go back."

She grunted. "Father Malloy is a right arse sometimes."

I snorted and covered my mouth. "Well," I sighed, lowering my hand. "He did tell me that she wasn't buried there. Now I have no idea where to search. Moira, I want to do what your grandmother said. Elspeth, she's..." I shuddered and absently reached up to touch the spot the bandage had been. Her eyes narrowed on the bruising there I couldn't hide with my hair. "She's dangerous. I am scared that she's going to hurt someone else. I'm scared to death that she is going to target Olivia or Isla next."

Finally, her eyes softened and she studied me. When her eyes returned to my bruise, she asked, "Did she do that to you?"

I nodded slowly. "She's attacked me a few times now. I think she knows I am trying to stop her, and she's trying to get rid of me before I can."

Moira uncrossed her arms and leaned back in her chair and stared off at the wall behind me. "Oh dear." I just sat there. Oh, dear was quite the understatement. She looked back at me after several long seconds. "I can't let you speak with my gran again. She's too frail as it is. Getting that worked up again wouldn't be good for her."

I nodded again glumly. I knew she was right, but I could feel my only hope slipping from my fingers.

"Look," she leaned forward, pressing her palms to the table. "If there is one thing that I am good at other than reshelving the same books over and over again, it's research. Give me some time. I will work whatever magic I have, and I will do my best to find the resting place of Elspeth Campbell. Okay?"

Hope bloomed as I smiled. "That would be wonderful. Thank you so much!"

"Hmmm, don't thank me yet, young lady. This village has done all they could to forget that woman ever existed. It won't be easy. Give me your number and when—if I find anything, I will give you a call. Yes?"

"Yes, ma'am." I could wait, it may not be patiently, but I could wait. "I appreciate it more than you could possibly know."

She grunted and pushed up from the table, going straight for the door and holding it open for me. "Yes, well, I'm not doing it for you. I'm doing it for those girls. No one wants to see the last of the Campbell line die with them."

It was harsh, but it was a reminder that they were it. After Ian's death, there were no more Campbells to carry on the name. I wondered what would become of the Manor if that should happen and shuddered. It wasn't a good thought.

After writing down my number for Moira at the circulation desk, I said my thank you's again and waved goodbye. All I could hope for was that Moira would be able to pull through for me.

I sat in the car, the trunk tied down with a bicycle crammed into it, hanging half out. As we drove back toward the Manor looming big and dark in the gloomy sky that hadn't lightened since I woke that morning, I thought of the journals again. The answer I needed was destroyed in some supernatural fire. Elspeth knew what I was doing, I was sure of it. I wondered if she had regained enough energy to come after me again yet, cold chills racing down my spine at the thought.

I hope you come back to me soon, Ian.

Twenty-Two

I spent the rest of the day in the conservatory, after convincing Olivia that it would be a fun place to hold our afternoon session. Honestly, I doubted Isla's claim that it was truly safe, but it was peaceful. It helped calm my nerves tremendously.

When the rain started, it rolled down the large panes of glass, obscuring the view of the outside world. It was loud with the pelting rain and I considered taking her back into the kitchen, but I couldn't bring myself to leave the room with the heavy, warm moist air. Since we couldn't talk over the sound of the driving rain, I peeled her an orange, and we both sat there smiling at each other while juice dripped from her chin.

After Chasity collected her, it gave me time to think. Wandering through the large room, I tried to clear my head from all thoughts of ghosts. I was staring out at a window, seeing nothing but water sliding down the panes, when I felt him. I didn't need to turn around.

When his arms came around me, I sighed and leaned back against him. "I missed you," I murmured, glad that the rain wasn't pounding as hard as it had been a short time ago. It was still fairly loud, but not too loud to speak. He nuzzled the top of my head, breathing deeply.

"I missed you, too, darling."

I turned around in his arms and wrapped mine around his waist. I stared up at his beautiful eyes. "I wish I knew where you went when you leave."

He grew thoughtful, a crease marring his perfect brows. *"I don't know. It's... noisy."*

I became confused. "Noisy? I thought you were in some kind of limbo state or something. What do you hear?"

"I swear, I can hear voices. Sometimes. Most of the time, I just hear sounds. I wish I could identify them, but it's too confusing." He shook his head. *"Let's not speak of that. There's nothing I can do about it. What about you? Have you been safe?"* He looked over my face as if he were looking for any sign of trauma.

"Yes. It's been quiet." I paused before telling him what happened today. Not because I didn't want him to know. It was just, I didn't have anything new yet. I had hope that Moira would be able to pull through for me, but until she did, I was going to try to keep my hopes from getting too high. "I went into the village today. I went back to the library to speak with Moira. At first I was going to ask to talk to her gran again, but she flat out refused. She did, however, promise to try to do her own research on where Elspeth might be buried."

"Ah, Moira. She's a gem. If she thinks that she can get information, then she is probably right." He rubbed my arms soothingly. *"Let her do her thing, I promise there's a reason that she is the village librarian."*

"Okay," I whispered.

"Come here." He took me by the hand and began leading me further into the corner of the room. The plants were denser, and the air seemed even thicker with moisture and the scent of rich soil. Once we reached the furthest corner, it felt as if we could have been the only ones in existence, completely cut off from any eyes and ears.

He pulled me into a little alcove set with a small table and a chaise lounge with thick cushions. A thin blanket was draped over the end and several small pillows were arranged at the top. It was perfect for a lazy afternoon of reading or just staring out at the garden outside. I still hadn't explored the grounds. They were so large and filled with rows of hedges and flowers, I was almost afraid I'd get lost. As it was, I still hadn't seen most of the inside of the Manor. I could probably live there for a year and still find something new to explore.

"This is so beautiful, Ian." I gasped at the intimate beauty of the quiet corner.

"It is."

I turned to face him but he wasn't looking at the space we were enclosed in. His eyes were fixed on me. I felt a blush creep up my cheeks at his intense perusal. I turned back to stare at the rain and fiddled with my fingers, finding it hard to withstand his stare.

I felt his hand cup my face, and he turned me back to face him again. I swallowed and blinked several times, and then my eyelids fluttered shut when he lowered his mouth to mine. The kiss he gave me was soft and gentle, making my heart sigh with happiness.

"I want nothing more than to love you, here, in this place. You look like an angel standing here."

His hands slid down my sides to my legs where he bunched the fabric of the sundress I wore. He slowly lifted it up over my hips then dipped down for another kiss. It was deeper than the last one, meant to build passion. It was working.

"Ian, I need you," I spoke softly against his lips, not wanting to break the spell that we seemed to be finding ourselves in.

"You have all of me, darling."

He tugged my dress up and over my head, leaving me in just my panties and bra. His eyes seemed to eat up every curve and dip of my body. With him staring at me that way, I didn't feel shy at all. I wasn't nervous, I was eager. I knew that in his arms I would experience the highest pleasure.

He stepped back and slipped his shirt over his head, letting it drop to the ground beside us. My eyes greedily drank up the view of his torso. The fact that he wasn't a solid form in front of me did nothing to lessen the effect he had on me.

"Ian," I asked as his hands went to his jeans. "I noticed that whenever you return, you don't have any injuries. That one time in the shower, she hurt you. But..." I reached out and ran my hand over his chest. "You are perfect."

He shrugged a shoulder as he slid his jeans down his thick thighs and goose bumps raised on my arms as I watched. He was all mine. *"I don't know. I'm just glad that I am able to do what is necessary to keep you safe from her."*

I bit my lip as I thought about my dream. "She was in my dream last night. I think... I think I died."

He froze for a second without looking up. I saw him clench his jaw and his hands tightened into fists. *"I hadn't heard of her attacking in dreams before."*

It was my turn to shrug. "It was terrifying. The Manor looked like it had been abandoned long ago. I thought about it. Like it hadn't changed in a long time. There were no skylights in the great hall. Do you think it was from her time? When the place was first built?"

"Perhaps." He pulled me close as he sank down onto the thick cushion and pulled me on top of him. *"No more talk of the witch. Right now, it's just you and me. Okay?"*

I bit my lip again and nodded. He was right. The only thing that mattered right now was the two of us. My legs straddled his hips, and he cupped my chin, leading my lips back to his. He started softly, teasing my mouth before the kiss turned hard, then desperate.

The rain started pouring down again, so hard that our moans couldn't be heard over the relentless pelting against the glass. But I felt them coming from me, and in the vibration of his chest. I felt the whisper of words I couldn't hear on my lips before he gripped the sides of my panties and pulled. Hard. A gasp left me as I felt a tugged on my skin and then nothing but warm air as the fabric was torn away.

His fingers delved down between us. Those fingers quickly sought my center, where he stroked through the wetness that was already there. I arched my neck as he let one of his fingers slide into me and he took advantage, licking my neck and then lightly biting there, making me jolt at the unexpected sensation. His tongue immediately soothed the small bite as his finger slid back out of me and went to my clit.

I cried out his name, uncaring that he couldn't hear me. He knew. He knew what he was doing to me as he continued to touch me there and his lips drifted downward until he found my breast. As he licked and sucked there, I felt him shift. Then finally, finally, he was inside me again. I could live a thousand lifetimes, and I knew I would always want him and no one else.

His hands gripped my hips as he pulled his mouth away with a final lick, and with nothing but his strength, he began to lift me and slide me back down. Over and over, he guided me the way he wanted as he filled me completely.

I could do nothing but hold on to his shoulders and allow him the control over my body. I rolled my head, barely able to keep my eyes open. When I glanced down at him with half-lidded eyes, it was to see him lost in his own pleasure. His jaw was clenched tight as he stared at me one moment and closed them tight the next, as if he could barely handle the feel of filling me.

When his arms began to tremble, I braced myself for better purchase on his shoulders and adjusted my legs. Then I took over. I moved my hips until I found the perfect movements, grinding my clit against him on the downward slide and tilting as I drew up. Every slide brought new sensations until I was so overwhelmed with the pleasure that my legs began to shake.

His hands tightened on my hips again and, though he didn't take over my movements, he began to add to them. He began to thrust up as I slid down and it soon became too much and I found myself screaming into our darkened corner, my head thrown back, my hair brushing his thighs.

I collapsed on top of him, sweaty and spent. I couldn't have moved a muscle, I was so exhausted. He buried his face into my hair that had fallen over my neck and, even though I couldn't hear it, I shivered as I felt the deep groan he let out as it vibrated my own chest.

We lay there together, reclined on the thick pillows of the chaise as the pounding of the rain drowned out our heavy breaths and just held each other tightly. He smoothed my hair back from my face and then resumed his nuzzle of my neck while his hands soothed me. He rubbed softly up and down, until I felt my eyes get heavy and my breaths began to even out.

When I woke, I was shivering, cold from the wind coming through the broken windowpane and freezing from the icy rain that was blowing inside, drenching me.

Twenty-Three

"Ian?" I whimpered, quickly realizing that I was once again alone. I glanced around, grabbing the soaked blanket at my feet and pulling it over me. It did nothing to stop the shivers that wracked my body. I clenched my jaw together hard, trying to stop them from chattering.

My eyes grew wide as I took in my surroundings. No longer was the cozy corner a safe and secluded spot. Everything around me was dark. The windows that once held back the rain were cracked and there were pieces of the broken glass missing, allowing the driving rain to enter, soaking everything.

The thick foliage of the plants that had hid the corner from view were gone. In its place were thorny vines. The thorns were long and looked wickedly sharp. They also surrounded me, trapping me inside unless I wanted to push my way through.

It had to be another dream. There was no other explanation that fit. But as I stood there miserable and frozen to my bones, I realized that it didn't feel like a dream. Last night held a strange quality to it. Even though I had been scared, somehow I knew none of it was real. This felt as real as it had felt making love to Ian in this very spot just a short time ago.

"Ian!" My scream was lost to the wind. Desperation clogged my throat while terror clawed at my insides. Then I froze, a shiver traveling up my spine that wasn't from the cold. I could hear the familiar sound of Elspeth's hateful screeching begin taking over the room.

I backed up until my knees hit the back of the lounge and fell heavily onto the soaked cushions. Water poured out onto the floor and drenched my feet, but that was the absolute least of my worries.

I scrambled up from the chair and ran to the thick, dangerous looking vines. The screams continued to echo and seemed to be getting closer.

"Ian!" I called out again. I wiped at the hot tears blurring my vision with frozen hands, though it did little to clear my eyes while the cold rain continued to drip from my hair down my face.

I reached for the vine closest to me, the smell of rot and decay filling the air as I gripped it. My stomach heaved at the stench. It reminded me of being in that room as the rotting body of Elspeth came towards me, intent on keeping me trapped with her forever. I cried out as the thorns dug deep into my palm.

I jerked back, the pain so intense I nearly doubled over. I cradled my hand to my chest and looked down at it. One of the massive thorns was stuck in the thicker part of my palm. As the rain washed away the blood, I could see black lines starting to spread from the wound. I yanked on the thorn and tossed it away from me and immediately blackness began to ooze like blood from the wound.

"No. No! Someone help me!" I backed away from the thorny vines as the screeching of the witch drew closer. She started to sound almost gleeful, like she knew she had me beat. I knelt down on the floor and huddled in on myself. I'd never been so scared before. Even when I was trapped in the room, I hadn't felt like this. I had Ian there to fight with me, to help me escape. At that moment, I had no one. I couldn't get through those vines unless I allowed myself to be torn to pieces by them.

Then I heard them. Dozens of voices. I couldn't make out what they were saying, but together, talking over each other, they were loud enough to hear over the rain and even over the screams. They sounded insistent, each of them demanding. Then the tone of the witch's screams changed. Elspeth was no longer gleeful. Instead, she sounded furious.

The louder the voices became, the more distant Elspeth seemed to be. As I lay there on the cold floor, squeezing my legs to my chest and my eyes closed, I began to wonder. Were the ghosts somehow protecting me? Were they keeping the witch away from me? Could they know I was close to setting them free? Somehow, they were intervening and trying to keep me safe so I could do what I had promised to do. I continued to cry, my sobs becoming ones of relief instead of terror.

"*Lacey?*" I heard Ian's voice as everything else went silent. I heard movement, the sound of ceramic hitting wood and then suddenly I was off the floor and in his arms and being carried.

He sat with me in his arms as I continued to shiver violently. I was no longer wet. The window was no longer broken, the leaves around us once again thick and lush. I shook my head and burrowed my head into his neck as I openly sobbed.

He rubbed my back soothingly without saying a word as I clung to him. That was the single most terrifying experience I had ever faced. I knew it wasn't a dream, even though it also seemed to not be real, either. I pulled back after a minute and held out my hand. There was no damage, no oozing black pus or even a red mark marring my skin, though the phantom pain was still there. Just like I still felt chilled to my bones.

He seemed to sense how cold I was as he tucked the blanket tight around me and rocked gently, soothing me as one might a young child. After holding me for a few minutes, I calmed and he finally broke.

"*Lacey, darling, you're scaring me. What happened?*"

I shook my head and sniffled, wiping my face on a corner of the thin cloth. "Elspeth. I don't know. She did something. It felt so real!"

"*I'm going to rip her fucking head off and shove it up her arse!*" His growled words made me giggle in spite of my lingering fear.

"I don't think it would actually do anything to stop her, but I'd love to see you give it a try." I sighed and laid my head against his broad shoulder and closed my eyes, suddenly very exhausted. "Can you take me to my bed?"

"*Of course, mo ghràidh.*"

He made sure the blanket was tucked securely around me and stood, gripping me tightly to him. Then I felt him dip down for a second and one of his hands leave me. A second later, a plate was set in my hands.

"I'm sorry I left you. I thought you might be hungry since you didn't have dinner."

On the plate was a delicious looking sandwich with thick slices of bread and piled high with meat and cheese. "Thank you so much," I whispered, my throat clogging at the thoughtful gesture. He just held me tighter and started to walk through the thick foliage.

"Anything for my darling girl."

I held the plate tightly and closed my eyes, hoping that we would make it to the room without being seen by anyone. I assumed that everyone was in bed or gone, though, or he wouldn't have gone into the kitchen in the first place.

I didn't open my eyes back up until he set me gently on the bed and drew the thick comforter around me.

"Are you feeling warmer?"

"Actually, yes." Warmth was finally starting to seep in and thaw my icy bones, though the occasional shiver still ran through me. I reached down and picked up the sandwich, having to open my mouth wide to be able to take a proper bite. I groaned at the delicious flavor. It was a perfect blend of meat, cheese, and condiments. "This is so good!" I mumbled around my mouthful and barely swallowed before chomping down on more. I hadn't realized just how famished I was.

After I had eaten half the sandwich and the edge of my hunger had been sated, I looked at Ian.

"You aren't hungry?"

He looked at me with amusement as I took one last bite before I decided I couldn't eat anymore of the delicious sandwich and set it on my nightstand. *"No, but I enjoyed watching you eat that tremendously."* His chuckle made me blush. *"Do you want a shower?"*

I shook my head. "No. I think I'll take one in the morning. I'm too tired to stand. Will you lay with me?"

"Of course I will."

I watched him strip for the second time that night and enjoyed it just as much as the first time. But I knew we wouldn't do anything more than hold each other tonight. I really was drained from my ordeal and from our earlier energetic activities.

We got comfortable under the covers, turned so my head was nestled in the crook of his arm.

Breathing a contented sigh, I told him how I was feeling. "I'm glad you're here with me." My whispered words floated in the dark, and his answering squeeze around my shoulder made me smile as I dozed off. I hoped that his presence would keep any bad dreams away and allowed myself to drift off to sleep.

That night, I dreamt of a future that was impossible.

Twenty-Four

Shocked violently out of my peaceful sleep, I sat straight up, my hand going to my chest. I glanced around as my heart rate began to slow and released a long sigh when I found I was alone. Although I really wanted to scream and cry, and throw an almighty tantrum, it would do no good. This was what I had to accept. There would be no morning cuddles or softly spoken good mornings.

Reluctantly, I threw the covers back and made my way into the bathroom. I turned on the shower, then sat on the toilet, contemplating the turn my life had taken in such a short time. In a way, I was proud of myself. I was far outside of my comfort zone. When I had accepted the position and agreed to fly across the ocean, I had expected for my life to remain much the way it had for the last ten years. Instead of hiding away from the world and only spending time with my one student, I was getting out, having an adventure. It was scary, and I didn't know if I would be able to complete my ultimate goal. But I was *living*. For the first time in my life, I was experiencing more than the same four walls.

I ducked under the hot spray and let the water cascade over me, imagining it was washing away the terror of yesterday. If only it could be that easy. As I scrubbed my body, I listened closely for any sounds from the preternatural world around me and sagged with relief when I didn't hear anything. Still, I didn't linger. I had never taken such quick showers in my life, and I was still fairly upset that baths were ruined for me. I missed having a good soak.

I had just turned off the shower and was wrapping the large fluffy towel around me when I heard my phone ringing next to the bed. I ran towards the bedroom, nearly falling on my ass when I slipped on my own puddle of water. I slapped the wet hair from my face and lunged for the phone before it could stop ringing. I had expected to see my mom's name on the display, or even my dad's, but I froze when I saw it was Moira.

"Oh, shit," I mumbled as the screen went black. I had been in so much shock at seeing her name, I hadn't answered. When it lit up and rang again in my hand, I startled, jumping a bit and nearly dropped the phone.

"Hello?" I asked cautiously once I connected the call.

"Lacey! I know where it is!"

I stood there in disbelief, staring at the blank wall, static filling my head. . She found it? She found the grave already? Was I prepared for this and what came next? My eyes shifted to the bed next to me and I stared down at the pillow that still had the indention where Ian had laid last night. Tears immediately filled my eyes and my nose began to sting.

"Lacey? Lacey, are you still there?" Moira's voice sounded like it was coming through a tunnel as the sight of the pillow became distorted from the moisture in my ears.

"I'm here," I mumbled.

"Oh, good. I thought I lost you there for a minute. Did you hear me? I found the grave!" Her excitement bleeding through the phone while I listened to her tell me how she traced back the generations of the locals, those who had families that had been living in the village the longest. "The Robertson's have been in these parts for centuries, so naturally, I asked them. But do you know what job their family usually held?"

I didn't answer her. I couldn't, I felt numb all over.

"They have always been the undertakers. The current Robertson's don't do that anymore. Their eldest son went to Uni for law instead and moved to Edinburg, but before he broke away from the family business and it was taken over by someone new, it had always been them. They were happy to talk about it. And, as luck would have it, their records weren't kept in the building that burned down like everything else.

"Lacey, they have *records*. Mr. Robertson was able to locate Elspeth Campbell's final resting place."

She paused, waiting for a response, but all I could do was make a strangled sound in my throat. That must have been enough for her to know that I was still listening because she gave me the news I desperately did not want to hear.

"They buried her out on the cliffs. Out behind the castle."

"The cliffs?" That was a big space, so many places. Perhaps it wouldn't be easy to find her grave afterall.

"Yes! There is a rock that was perfect for a monument, so that's where she was buried. It isn't marked, but it is easy to find."

My shoulders sagged in defeat.

"All you need to do is go behind the castle ruins and look for a rock that is standing up in the shape of a headstone. She is buried there."

She became silent, all I could hear were her breaths as she had finally expelled all her excitement. "Thank you, Moira. I really appreciate your help with this." It was a lie, every word. I suddenly wished I had never asked her for help. When she said she was good at research, I hadn't anticipated that it would take her less than twenty-four hours.

Her tone softened as she spoke quieter. "Oh, sweetheart." I sniffled and knew I had to end the call.

"I have to go. Thank you, though, really."

"Okay, Lacey. Let me know if you need some help, okay?" She paused and then said, "You don't have to do this, you know. Or if you want someone to go with you…"

"No," I cut her off. If I was going to complete this task, it was going to be just me. I wasn't going to involve anyone else. "It's fine. I can do it. Thank you, though."

"Alright. Goodbye, Lacey."

"Bye, Moira."

I dropped the phone to the bed and stood there staring down at it, my hair leaving droplets of water on the sheet and the dark face of the phone. I looked up at the window, but the curtains were fully closed for once. I couldn't determine if it was another stormy day that would prolong what I would have to do, or if it was bright and sunny out.

On wooden legs, I walked over to the window, letting the towel slip through my fingers and drop to the floor. I pulled back the heavy drapes and looked out into the bright light of the morning. Then, after I closed the drapes again, I walked over to the wardrobe and began to dress for the day, slipping on a pair of jeans and a comfortable sweater.

I had a little girl to teach.

***

ALL DAY I felt like I was in a fog. I smiled at Olivia and praised her efforts as she worked on her numbers. I ate lunch, though I couldn't have told anyone what it was in front of me. After Isla got home from work at the bank, dressed in her fashionable clothes and beautiful high-heeled shoes, we all ate dinner together before parting ways.

The entire time, I felt detached and out of focus.

When evening fell, I walked up the stairs to my room and changed out my flats for a pair of tennis shoes. I grabbed my small backpack and emptied it out on the bed. Then I went into the bathroom and brushed back my hair, pulling it into a tight ponytail.

I stood at the mirror for a few long minutes, just staring. I didn't see myself as I was, I was seeing myself as I could have been. The dreams that had been flitting through my head all day. Dreams that I would be killing tonight.

Ian had promised me that he would find a way to stay. I swallowed hard, a lump getting stuck in my throat. I turned on the cold water and pushed the sleeves of my sweater up to my elbows so I could splash the water on my face.

He promised. But it wasn't a promise that was his to make. He didn't control the curse. Elspeth did. And what I was preparing to do tonight would end her reign once and for all.

I dried my face and rested my hands against the countertop, hanging my head. I took several deep breaths in and out, and did my best to ignore the whispers that had been growing steadily louder throughout the day.

The ghosts knew.

They had been active while I was in both the morning and afternoon session with Olivia. During dinner, they had been practically in my ear. They knew it was time, and they were excited. What I hadn't heard all day was the witch, and that scared me. I was terrified that she was saving up all her energy for what was coming.

Elspeth was going to do everything within her power to stop me. Of that, I had no doubt.

I straightened up and didn't bother to look at myself as I left the bathroom. I grabbed the jacket I had left on the end of the bed, along with the backpack and shrugged it on. I took the bag by one of the straps and carried it out the door with me and down to the kitchen as my footsteps echoed loudly in the great hall.

I rummaged through the pantry until I found what I was looking for. A large box of salt next to flour and sugar bags. I picked up its heavy weight and slid it into the bag. The next thing I went looking for, I found easily enough. There were fireplaces everywhere in a house this large. Most of them had long wooden matchsticks for lighting the fires. I took a box and slid it into the bag with the salt, then slid the back pack over my shoulders, letting the weight settle against my lower back.

I started to walk toward the front door, then stopped. I would need light. I bit my lip as I thought about where I would find a flashlight, but I had no idea where to start looking. I decided to head out to the garage until I found a shovel and hoped I would find one along the way. If I had no other option, I could always resort to using my phone for light.

I quietly pulled the heavy door open and closed it softly behind me, slipping out into the darkening night. I stopped and looked up at the sky to see the moon was out and it was full. Well, that was one thing that I would have going for me. With the bright light of the moon, I should be able to see well enough to not fall over the cliff.

I rounded the corner of the Manor, walking toward where I had seen a large shed. I was sure it wasn't the garage. The garage was likely huge, but maybe it was exactly what I needed in order to find a shovel. As I approached, I could tell I was right, it wasn't the garage. I didn't know what the building was. It was too big to be a simple garden shed, though.

I hesitantly turned the knob, relieved when the door swung open easily. Once my eyes adjusted to the darkness, I gasped. It was a workshop! I pulled my phone out of my pocket to turn the light on and swung it around me. The room was filled with wooden furniture in different stages of completion. Someone worked with wood and they were damn good at it.

I ran a hand over a bookshelf with intricate designs on the edges, the wood so smooth it felt like satin under my fingertips. Somehow I knew this was Ian's workshop. I could feel him here. It was something we had never talked about, what his life was like before he died. I didn't know what he did for a living. I wondered now if this was a hobby, or if he made a living off his craft.

I walked over to see a half finished cradle and wondered who it would have been for and if they were sad that they would never get to place their child in it.

I was about to leave when I swept my phone over the whole place one last time and saw in the back corner exactly what I had been looking for.

Twenty-Five

I never did find a flashlight. However, I did find an old-fashioned lantern that had just a little bit of oil left in it. I figured it would make a good fuel source, but there wasn't enough to waste. I wouldn't be able to use the lantern as a light source if I were going to use it later to burn the body. I certainly couldn't waste any more time searching for a flashlight, since the voices that only I seemed to be able to hear all day were getting louder, pressing me forward with urgency.

I was going to try to ride my new bike up the trail to the ruins, but I thought of the uneven terrain and how difficult it would be on a good day. Balancing the heavy shovel I'd found while riding a bike when I hadn't been on one in ages seemed like a recipe for disaster. So, I trudged up the long path on foot, using only the moonlight to guide me. Well, the moon and the voices that wouldn't stop.

When I came to the first large portion of fallen wall, I stopped and considered my choices. I thought about climbing over them. I knew the ground mostly evened out once I was past the worst of the crumbling rock. But then I would have to find my way out the other side. I hadn't made it that far in my exploration last week. I had no idea if there was even a way out. So around I had to go.

It was going to take me even longer without cutting through the rubble and there was still the unknown, but I figured if I walked straight to the cliffs, I would be able to follow along the edge until I came along the back of the castle.

The air was chilly but after dragging the shovel and having the heavy weight of my backpack resting against the back of my jacket was making me uncomfortably warm, while at the same time, my fingers were chilled. Not to mention my nose.

I could hear the angry waves crashing below, and as I got closer to the cliff edge the wind started to pick up, grabbing strands of my hair and ripping them out of the ponytail. I had to stop and tuck the end of my hair down into my jacket to keep from being slapped in the face.

I glanced up at the moon nervously the closer I got to see clouds moving in, beginning to cover portions of the light, turning the night progressively darker. I didn't know how I would be able to do this without being able to see properly. I started cursing at myself for not waiting another day, for not asking Isla for a day off from teaching Olivia. I was sure she would have understood if I explained the situation to her. But I knew the ghosts would never have let me rest if I hadn't come out here tonight.

I finally saw the edge of the cliff and stood there for a moment, staring out at the sea far below. It looked dangerous. The waves crashing so hard against the rocks that it almost sounded like thunder. I could almost picture what it would be like to tumble over the side. The fall would be terrifying, but the landing would be devastating. There was no surviving a fall like that.

I took hold of the shovel again and turned toward the back of the castle. I was close. The height of the ruins loomed over the area and the space where the grave was supposed to be was nearly covered in complete darkness. I looked around on the ground for any stray pieces of wood I could find, hoping there would be enough that wasn't saturated from yesterday's storm. I needed enough dry pieces that would allow me to build a small fire. I would need the light while I dug the grave.

I took my bag off and turned it around, putting my arms back through the straps and unzipped the opening. Then as I walked, I picked up any small sticks or branches I could find. Luckily, most of them seemed to have dried out well during the sunny day we'd had. Unfortunately, there wasn't a whole lot of wood to be found. The trees were sparse up on the cliffs. What was there was small and twisted from the wind and rocky terrain.

I had to take my phone out and use the light before I could go any further. I looked up to see that the moon was nearly eclipsed by the cloud cover. A strong breeze made me shiver as I reached down to pick up another small branch that was wedged between two rocks.

The further I got to the ruins, the deeper the darkness became, until the moon didn't even matter any more. It wouldn't have made a difference if there were no clouds at all. The shadow from the castle was too thick for any moonlight to reach.

My bag was pretty full when I came to a dead stop. In front of me was a rock that couldn't be mistaken. I swept my light over the stone and wondered at how nature could have carved something so perfect for a headstone.

Without taking my eyes off the stone, I lay the shovel on the ground and slid the straps of my bag off my shoulders. There was something ominous about this stone. It fairly vibrated with a menacing energy. It was as if her aura had leached into the space around her. I shivered at the thought that she had infected the very ground I was standing on.

I quickly pulled out all the wood I had gathered and was disappointed at the small pile. It had seemed like so much more when it was stuffed in my bag. But now that it was laid out on the ground, I could see there was hardly enough for a small fire. I had no choice, though. It would have to make do.

I arranged the pieces as best as I could several feet away from the grave. I was trying to remember what my dad had taught me the few times we had gone camping when I was a kid. I pulled the long box of matches from the bottom of the bag and lit one, insanely happy when the wood began to smoke. It didn't catch fire, though. I was about to give up hope and light another match when it had almost reached my fingertips, when a spark and flame caught. I startled, falling back on my rear, then nervously laughed at myself. Everything about this night was making me jumpy.

I watched as the fire continued to grow. It was small, but it gave off a decent amount of light and just a small bit of warmth. I turned back to look at the grave as I turned the light from my phone off and slid it back into my pocket.

"Alright, Elspeth. I think it's time. What do you think?"

It was entirely the wrong thing to say. An angry shriek pierced through the night, making me realize, for the first time since I had found the grave, that the voices of the ghosts had quieted.

"Shit. Okay." I took a deep breath and hung my head, trying to shore up my failing courage. I was in a spooky place, ready to do something morally questionable, completely away from any other living being. If I didn't get this done quickly, I was probably fucked.

I straightened my shoulders back and picked up the shovel. With both hands gripping the handle tightly, I slammed the end into the ground, watching as it sank in about two inches. I blew out a breath, and with one last mental pep talk, I placed my shoe on the shovel and pressed. Hard.

It sank in a couple more inches, and then I scooped, beginning a pile to the side. I was a couple feet from the headstone, about where a waist would be. I figured there was no right way to dig up the grave of a murderess witch. Starting in the middle was as good as any other place.

With each press and scoop I grew tired, hot, and sweaty. I had to take off my jacket at one point because it was hindering my movements. By the time the hole was about four feet wide and about a foot deep, my hands were aching and blisters were forming. The angry shrieks were also getting louder and more desperate. But the worst part, my fire was nearly burned out completely.

I was a failure at this.

"Darling, would you like some help?"

I whirled around, so beyond grateful to hear Ian's voice that I nearly laughed. I would have if the situation weren't so dire.

"Ian!" I looked at the pitiful hole I had managed to dig. "I didn't realize how difficult it would be to dig up a grave." I shrugged one aching shoulder.

He stepped into me and with one hand he took the shovel, the other he placed on my waist. He leaned down and brushed a soft kiss across my lips. *"I'm sorry I'm late. I've got it from here."*

I sagged in relief and stepped back from his touch reluctantly. I moved around the stone to lean against it, truly not giving one single shit if it was disrespectful. I was tired, and it was her fault, anyway.

I pulled my phone out and shone the light into the hole I had already dug so Ian could see.

"It's been very noisy today," I said conversationally as I watched him toss to the side a shovelful of dirt three times the size of the ones I had done. "I think the ghosts are excited. They somehow knew something was up." I looked at his handsome face, mostly hidden in shadows. "Did you feel anything today?"

He paused briefly before continuing at a much quicker pace than I had been able to work. At the rate he was going, he'd have the grave completely uncovered in just a few minutes.

"No," he said after a long moment. *"I didn't sense anything at all."*

The way he said it sounded like there was a little more than he was telling me. I allowed him his silence as he worked. I couldn't help but admire his show of strength.

"Ian," I called out softly. I was afraid to ask, not because I thought I would offend him, or afraid of the answer, but because I didn't want to upset him or make him sad by reminding him of his life. "I found a workshop tonight. There were amazing and beautiful wood pieces in there. Was it yours?"

I watched as he slammed the shovel hard into the dirt and then leaned a forearm on the handle. He looked at me. I couldn't see his green eyes clearly unless I pointed the light at him, but I knew they were intense and right on me.

"Woodworking." He shook his head and then grabbed the shovel again, getting right back to work. "Wood is... was my passion. I spent years doing what was expected of me. I ran the family business, kept the village running properly, and acted as the proper Lord I was raised to be. But whenever I had a spare moment, I had a piece of wood in my hand."

"Those pieces, the bookshelf, the cradle?"

"You want to know if they were commissions?" I nodded, even though he couldn't see me. He jumped down into the hole and began heaving out big shovelfuls of dirt. *"No, darling. I couldn't take commissions since I never knew what my schedule would allow. Those pieces would have been*

picked up by a shop owner from Edinburg. Any proceeds I made on the pieces he sold were donated to the village food bank."

"That's amazing. But I hate that you couldn't just do what you truly loved to do. Why couldn't you be a proper Lord and still work on your wood pieces? I saw them, Ian. They were amazing. I bet they go for crazy high prices."

He grunted in response but didn't answer. It didn't matter anyway. The time for talking was over. He had hit wood.

Twenty-Six

"*Fuck!*" Ian's deeply growled curse had me jerking my wide eyes from the bottom of the hole up to his face to find him staring over my shoulder. I jerked around, my heart racing, just in time to see the witch reach out and swipe a hand at my face. Her jagged, talon-like fingernails were curved, and her face was twisted in a fury that made my blood run cold.

I had no time to do anything but raise my arm in defense to protect my face. I cried out as her vicious claws raked down my forearm. A burning pain raced up my arm as she slashed deep groves, cutting through my sweater. I cradled my arm to my chest just as a blur of movement raced past me and Ian's body rammed into hers, sending her flying back.

Screams of outrage filled the night as I watched the two ghostly figures wrestling each other. Ian punched her in the face, causing her head to fly back, but all she did was lift it right back up to sneer at him as if it hadn't affected her at all. She raised her hand again, and I watched as she swiped at his throat.

At the last second, he jerked and her claws missed their mark, instead raking down his chest. The night was as black as his shirt so I couldn't see any blood, but she left jagged grooves in the cloth. I didn't know if she could hurt him in his state, not permanently at least, but just the thought of seeing the man I loved with his throat brutally torn out was enough to make me reach out to try to help. He grabbed her hand before she could try again.

He turned his head to look at me standing there, trembling, with my hand outstretched towards them. He was gripping her wrist with one hand and holding her close to him with another, his hand wrapped securely around her frail looking bicep and he held her in place.

"Hurry, get to the bones!" His barked demand had my arm dropping and taking a step back. I didn't want to leave him to fight her alone, but I was of no help in a fight like that. He waited for my nod of agreement, then turned back to her, pushing her further away from the grave and me.

I quickly scrambled into the hole, ignoring the dirt that was clinging to me and coating my bleeding wound. I reached down and grabbed the wooden boards that made up her coffin and started pulling. It was easier than I had expected. Nearly two hundred years underground had made it weak and rotted.

The wind began to howl, battling for supremacy with the outraged screams and grunts of the two ghosts fighting just yards away from where I was. It seemed to almost dive down into the hole, blinding me with swirling dirt and the hair from my ponytail whipping wildly into my face.

I tried to ignore it. Needing to keep my focus, I had to ignore the pain of the slashes on my arm, the splinters of wood that dug into my hands as I yanked and threw rotted pieces of wood to the side. I had to ignore everything but getting inside the wooden coffin and to the bones. But my mind was in chaos and my heart was beating so hard I could hear it pounding in my ears.

When most of the wood was torn away, I could finally see what lay beneath and had to hold back the vomit that made its way up my throat. The bones were covered in dirt but still clearly visible, their paleness almost seeming to glow amongst the darkness at the bottom of the grave.

I pushed back away from the remains and held my hand to my mouth to hold back my gag before I realized that I just put grave dirt on my face. I immediately turned around and desperately clawed my way out of the open hole.

I crawled away on my hands and knees, heaving from the effort of holding back my panic. I could barely hear over the howling wind and couldn't see much past the hair in my eyes. I stumbled to my feet and over to the headstone where my phone was still resting. It had shifted from the wind, and was no longer fully lighting the grave.

I rubbed my hand on my jeans, attempting to get as much of the filth off as possible before picking up my phone. Then, taking a deep breath to brace myself, I shone the light into the grave to make sure enough of Elspeth's skeleton was uncovered. The last thing I wanted to do ever again was to have to climb back down into that hole with the witch's remains.

The light passed over her head, illuminating empty eye sockets half filled with dirt, a jaw no longer attached to the rest of the skull. A ribcage that almost seemed like it had collapsed in on itself. I couldn't make out the pelvis, but could easily see the pale bones of her legs. It looked like most of the body was uncovered. Thankfully, not much of the dirt that Ian had shoveled out had fallen back in to cover her after I removed the wood.

A loud screech jerked me from my investigation of the bones. Though I swept the light across the darkness, I couldn't see where Ian was. I wanted to call out to him, but was worried that distracting him would be disastrous for us all.

I looked around for my backpack and found it resting by the long dead fire. With jerky movements, I managed to pull out the box of salt with one hand and carried it over to the hole. As I struggled to peel the sticker sealing the spout, the wind seemed to attack me. I nearly fell back into the hole as a gust of strong wind pummeled me and I had to drop the box to brace myself as it seemed to shove against me.

Once it let up, I picked up the salt again, setting down my phone so I could use both hands. As soon as I got the label peeled back, I pulled the spout too hard, making it pop out of the box completely. I grabbed my phone and started to get to my feet when another gust of wind, even stronger than the first, hit me square in the back. I nearly dropped the salt into the grave as I threw my hands forward to catch myself and watched as my phone skittered away from me, over the bumpy ground and plummeted into the darkness.

Thunder cracked, seeming right overhead, making me jump so hard I almost followed after my phone. I knew I was going to regret it in the morning, but I just couldn't bring myself to retrieve it. I carefully sat back up and pulled the box of salt over to me. Some had spilled, but it was still mostly full and I knew it would have to do.

I stood up, planting my feet to find purchase against the violent wind, and precariously leaned over the hole. The light from my phone was shining over the eerie, open eye sockets of the skeleton, and I had to hold back another shudder of revulsion. Being careful not to waste any salt on the dirt instead of where it needed to go, I began to shake the box, starting at the head.

I watched as the salt cascaded down onto the bones and nearly laughed when I realized that the wind was actually helping it land where it was needed the most. I slowly walked down the length of the hole using every single last grain of salt until the skeleton was covered from head to toe.

A screech suddenly sounded so close to me that I jerked my head up. Ian had both arms wrapped tight around Elspeth as she dragged him closer to the grave. I could just make out their figures in what little light there was. It looked like they'd had quite a fight, both of them were bloody and their clothing was torn. I swallowed hard, blinking away the tears that wanted to fall.

Not able to take any more time, I turned away from the sight and searched the ground for the lantern. I could barely see anything on the ground and stumbled over to where I knew I had left my bag. My foot kicked something, and I heard glass break.

"Damn it!" I dropped to my knees and scooped up the lantern, slicing my finger on a jagged piece of glass. "I just want to end this already!" I screamed into the black void of the sky, so frustrated and emotionally overwrought. I honestly didn't think I could take any more, but didn't want to give up. I couldn't give up.

I reached out blindly for my backpack and snatched up the strap, dragging it to me, and stumbled to my feet with the broken lantern as the wind continued to howl furiously around me. The sounds of screaming and grunting were getting closer, and I didn't know how much fight Ian had left in him.

I practically ran back to the grave and carefully tipped the lantern over, relieved to see there was still some oil left inside after being knocked over. It didn't cover much, just a line down the left side of the bones, but it had to be enough. I tossed the lantern in the hole with my phone and dug inside the bag for the long box of matches.

One by one, I struck a match, only to have the wind blow it out before it could do more than flicker.

"Please, please, please," I cried, exasperated tears finally falling. I was out of options. I had nothing else to light the fire with. If I couldn't get a match to flame, we were all utterly fucked.

Suddenly, Elspeth was right on the other side of the grave. Her arm stretched impossibly far to reach for me. She was floating, not needing to stand on the ground. I fell back on my ass, desperately moving backwards, trying to put distance between us. Ever my protector, Ian was there to yank on one of her arms, keeping her from reaching me.

Then, as I stared in disbelief, ghosts began appearing, seemingly out of nowhere. So many of them materialized next to and around Ian, I could barely see him through the mass of translucent bodies. They looked different from him, more incorporeal while he was now nearly solid. As I watched, they all began to grab at the witch and as one started dragging her backward away from me and away from the hole.

I took it as my opportunity to try the matches again. This time, I huddled up against the headstone, using it as a buffer against the wind. If it didn't work, my only recourse would be to climb down into the grave. But I shook that thought away. I couldn't do it. I couldn't put myself down there again. Not with the fire. Not with the chance that I might get trapped. Burning alive? No, I just couldn't do it.

I wiped my face on my shoulder and looked in the box. I only had a few matches left. I glanced up to see the group had successfully dragged Elspeth close to the edge of the cliff. I grabbed a match and bent my body over it, and struck.

I watched hesitantly as it flickered, then flared. Triumphant, I wanted to jump up and yell the way Tom Hanks had in 'Castaway', proud that I had created fire. I held it a moment longer as the flame licked at the wood, burning brightly. Then, cupping my hand over it until the last second, I dropped it.

My heart sank as I watched it fizzle out, and I began mentally preparing myself for the worst-case scenario. Because I knew there was only one way this would work. As much as the thought of climbing into the witch's grave and lighting her skeleton on fire with me in it terrified me, I wouldn't walk away from this night a failure.

Then, as I wiped my eyes again on my shoulder, I saw a faint wisp of smoke, then a spark. As the oil caught, the flame raced down the length of the skeleton where I had poured the line of oil. Watching it burn a trail, the flames seemed to gain strength, or there was more to salting a witch's bones than I had expected because suddenly the fire flared so brightly blue flames engulfed the whole grave.

I fell back with a gasp, unable to take my eyes away from the sight. Until the screams of outrage I had been hearing all night changed their tone. I looked up to see Elspeth writhing in the grasp of Ian and at least a dozen ghosts with several more standing there watching. Her cries turned to ones of agony, as if she were the one being burned.

I jumped up as I watched the group get to the edge of the cliff. Then, as one, they all toppled over together. I reached out a hand as if I could stop Ian from falling with them, but there was nothing I could do but watch helplessly. With my own scream of agony, I saw his eyes as they bore into mine.

His eyes spoke the words he couldn't. Everything he wanted to say, but hadn't had the chance to yet. Every tender, loving thing he had already said. All I could do was stand there and scream in denial as he disappeared, along with every ghost. Those who hadn't been a part of the huddle turned back to me as if to say thank you. Then, they turned and together, stepped off the side of the cliff, disappearing from sight. The vicious wind stopped, the night now silent, and I knew it was over.

I sat down heavily, my cries cutting off completely, and stared blankly into the dissipating fire below. I couldn't say how long I sat there. I was numb to everything. I couldn't feel the cold, couldn't feel the cuts on my arms and hands. My mind was blank.

The fire dimmed and then went out completely, startling me from my haze. Blindly, I got to my feet and started walking. I vaguely realized that I could see my surroundings, the clouds clearing when Elspeth disappeared along with the wind. I slowly trudged back to the house, leaving behind everything I had begun the night with.

I tried not to think. I knew, just knew, that if I allowed one thought in, it would all come crashing down on top of me and I would break. So, I took it one step at a time. By the time I made it to the front door, the sky was turning gray at the edges. I didn't want to see the sunrise. I didn't want to know that a new day would start without Ian. I didn't want to believe that life was just supposed to go on with the sun rising and setting every day as though this had never happened. All I wanted to do right then was climb into my bed and pretend that it hadn't.

I slipped off my filthy shoes and carried them through the house. They were going into the garbage, along with everything else I was wearing. Then, I was going to take a long hot shower. And I was going to keep pretending.

Twenty-Seven

I woke up to the sound of knocking at my door. I groggily reached for my phone to check the time when the memories of last night hit me hard. I choked back a sob, refusing to let it out. I couldn't, not now knowing I would have to face whatever was at the door.

I cracked open the door to see Chasity standing there in her perfectly pressed clothing, looking irritated until she got a good look at me. Her words faltered in the process of asking me what the hell I was doing still in bed instead of downstairs with Olivia.

"Are you alright, miss?" Her concerned tone almost made me crack, but I straightened my shoulders.

"I'm sorry. I—I had a bad night. If you give me five minutes, I can be downstairs to start the lesson."

"Uh, if you don't mind me saying, you should probably take the day off. You don't look well."

I hesitated. I needed to do what I was being paid generously for, but...

"Really, miss. I will take care of Miss Olivia today. If you'd like, I can clear it with Madam Isla, but I'm sure she would want you to rest."

All I could do was nod my agreement. She gave me a small smile, the first I had seen from her, and bobbed her head before turning away. I closed the door and slumped against it. I walked into the bathroom to throw some water on my face and saw the dirty clothes in a heap on the floor. Ignored them and walked to the sink, refusing to look in the mirror.

After taking care of my needs and splashing cold water on my face, I wasn't feeling any more awake than I had before. I stumbled back into my bed, pulling the covers up to my chin, willing myself to forget. I rolled over until I was facing away from the pillow Ian had used, wanting to keep ignoring the reality of the situation, but the hollowness in my chest had me reaching up to rub there until I finally reached behind me. I held his pillow close to my body, inhaling the scent that wasn't even there. At the thought of not even having that to comfort me, I squeezed my eyes shut tight and just breathed.

The second time a knock woke me up, I cracked my eyes open, looking at the sliver of light I could see through my drapes, and sighed. I had slept the entire day away. I stumbled from the bed, righting my sleep shorts and shirt as I made my way to the door. As soon as I opened it, Isla's concerned face greeted me. Maybe it was because she shared Ian's eyes, maybe it was just because she looked truly concerned. Whatever it was, the walls I had tried to build since walking away from the cliffs began to crack.

"Oh, darling girl." Her words were the final blow to my composure. As my face crumpled and the tears started falling, she closed the door and led me over to the bed and pulled me down with her. She held me tight and whispered as she glided her hand over my hair soothingly.

"You did it, didn't you? Sent her away?" All I could do was nod. "And Ian's gone now." It wasn't a question, she could see the devastation written all over me, but I still nodded anyway. She hitched in a breath and let it out raggedly as she began to cry with me.

We lay there for what could have been hours as she comforted me the way only a mother could, as we both mourned a man that we loved in different ways.

After I was calmed enough to speak, I told her everything that had happened since the moment I had arrived. I told her of the journals and of the visit to the village. The library and Moira's gran that had given me the knowledge of what to do. I told her of Ian, of how it started as him being my protector, but of becoming so much more. It didn't chase away the pain, but it helped to tell someone that knew him and wouldn't judge me. There were few people in the world that would believe my story and I knew that I wouldn't be able to share the truth with anyone else. My parents would think I was crazy. They wouldn't understand how I had fallen in love so deeply, so quickly with a man that was already dead.

She convinced me to go downstairs with her to have a sandwich, and as I ate the food that looked so mouthwatering on the plate but tasted like ash on my tongue, I recounted the events on the cliffs.

After we ate, she insisted on taking a look at my wounds that I had wrapped carelessly with the supplies I had found in my bathroom and clucked her tongue at the damage. I allowed her to rewrap it properly, ignoring her threats of sending me back to the doctor.

"It will be fine."

She didn't appreciate my mumbled excuses, but allowed me my denials.

"Tomorrow I will take the day off. You and I and Olivia will have a wonderful girl's day."

I started to shake my head. I would never be comfortable doing the things she did with Olivia. The thought of having to sit in front of a stranger as she worked on my fingers was enough to have my anxiety spike, even after all I had been through since my arrival.

"Shhh, no. We will stay here. We can sit in the movie room and watch whatever you want. As long as it is appropriate for a six-year-old, of course." She winked at me, causing a smile to almost break free.

"You have a movie room?"

Her laughter filled the kitchen as she replied, "Oh, sweetheart, you really haven't explored much of your home, have you?"

I swallowed hard and looked up at her from where I had been staring at my glass of orange juice. "I can stay?" I hadn't thought she would kick me out, but it was such a strange situation.

She reached across the table and grabbed my hand, holding tightly. "Of course." Her tone was firm and serious. "This is your home for as long as you want it. There will always be a place for you here. You saved it, Lacey. You saved my Olivia. I owe you more than I could ever repay.

And no, my offer is not out of gratitude. You earned it." She paused and took a stuttering breath before pasting a bright smile on her face. "Ian would want you here."

My choked out, "Thank you," was the only thing I could say to her heartfelt words. I quickly excused myself to head back upstairs.

***

THE NEXT THREE days were a mixture of happiness at feeling like I was truly a part of their little family, and heartbreak that I could never completely hide.

We had done exactly as Isla had promised and spent a relaxing day watching children's movies and eating junk food. I let Olivia paint my fingernails in every color of polish she owned and loved every minute of it.

We all tried to get back to a place of normalcy. Isla and I did our best to keep up a good face for Olivia, not wanting her to know that anything monumental had changed. But little children aren't oblivious to the world around them.

"The ghosts are gone."

I froze as I was pointing to a word that I was having her sound out for me. My hand started shaking, and I quickly pulled it into my lap.

"They are?" I tried to keep my voice even, but I knew I wasn't fooling her.

She just nodded her head as she stared down at the page of words. "Yes. I don't hear them anymore."

I just smiled shakily and whispered, "That's good, sweetheart."

She smiled up at me, her adorable crooked smile. "Yes. They wanted to go home and now they are." She looked back down at the paper and said, "I'm glad."

"So am I, sweetie."

***

. . .

Later that evening we were sitting at the table eating a lovely dinner of pot roast as Olivia had Isla and I laughing at her attempts at cracking jokes.

"Knock, knock!" She called out.

Both Isla and I answered with a swift, "Who's there?"

"Boo!"

"Boo, who?"

"You don't have to cry, it's only a joke!" She erupted into little girl giggles that were infectious. Both of us couldn't help but laugh along with her.

Isla bopped her on the nose. "Very clever, my love."

The sound of a phone ringing had us all freezing. Isla looked over to the phone that was mounted to the wall. In all the time I had been there, I had never heard it ring. I hadn't even realized that it worked at all. As she got up to answer it, I cringed. I still hadn't replaced my phone. I had sent my mom an email explaining that it had been damaged beyond repair and had promised to replace it soon. I hadn't even attempted to find out what the process would be to get another phone yet.

Isla's high-pitched words had me twisting in my seat to give her my full attention.

"What do you mean? That's not possible!"

I glanced over at Olivia to see her staring, her eyes wide at her mother's obvious stress.

"Okay, I will be there as soon as I can!"

Isla slammed the phone down and ran into the great hall, and screamed for Chasity.

"Yes, madam?" She stood at the top of the stairs, wringing her hands in front of her.

"I need you to care for Olivia. I don't know how long I might be gone. It could be a few days." Without waiting for a response, she ran back into the kitchen and grabbed her purse that she had left sitting at a side table.

"Mommy?" Olivia's little voice wavered, upset at the strange way her mother was acting.

"I will be back soon, I promise, love. Be good for Chasity." She leaned down and kissed the top of Olivia's head. She gave me a strange look before turning to leave quickly, nearly knocking into Chasity as she came into the room.

As I sat there dumbfounded, Chasity sat down in the abandoned chair and placed an arm around the crying Olivia, attempting to comfort her.

I stared at the empty doorway and listened as the front door slammed shut. Isla, and any explanation for her sudden departure, gone in an instant.

Twenty-Eight

Isla ended up being gone for four days. During that time, Chasity and I did our best to keep Olivia distracted. We spent a lot of time playing with dolls with her and watching movies. We didn't know how to answer any of her questions. Most of them were her wanting to know how long her mother would be gone.

On the fourth day, we were walking to the kitchen to prepare lunch together when we heard the door open. We all turned to stare until we saw Isla enter with someone standing behind her that I couldn't see.

Olivia's scream of, "Mam!" echoed around us as she hurried forward as fast as her little crutches could carry her. When Isla stepped forward to greet her, she revealed the man behind her, leaning heavily against the door.

I took in his large frame, dark hair and large smile. When his mossy green eyes met mine across the large space, I felt my head swim. I had spent the last week trying to learn to live with a gaping hole in my chest. It was a hole I knew would never be filled ever again.

I caught myself on the doorframe to the kitchen, as I felt my knees go weak. Still, I couldn't look away from those eyes. I hadn't realized that my breath was coming in shallow pants until Chasity reached out to touch my arm.

"Miss Lacey, are you okay?"

I couldn't hear my raspy pants over the ringing in my ears. I had to be seeing things. None of this was real. I had to be imagining that he was standing there, in the Manor, *alive*. As my vision began to dim, I saw his eyes widen in alarm and the smile he had been wearing dropped. I could tell he was saying something, but my mind had already shut down.

***

Hushed voices sounded like they were coming through a heavy fog. I was propped up against something hard and someone's fingers were drifting through my hair. I lay there for a minute, trying to get my bearings. My mind was denying what I had seen. As soon as the memories surfaced and I registered who was holding me, I sat up. I looked around the room and realized we were in the study near the front of the great hall. I had never been inside this room before, but I had seen through the open door as I had passed by when someone was inside dusting. Isla was in the room, but thankfully Olivia was nowhere in sight to see my impending freak out.

I scrambled to my feet and swayed as soon as I was upright. Hands reached out to steady me, but I batted them away. I whirled around and fixed my wide eyes on the man and narrowed them. I pointed a shaky finger in his face as he leaned forward, ready to catch me if I fell. My heart gave a little lurch, but I tamped it down.

"You," I accused, glaring at him. My nose was stinging with the tears I ruthlessly held back with all my strength. "You're dead. I watched you f—fall." My breath hitched with my words. We all knew I wasn't referring to the act that caused him to be what I had believed to be a ghost. I swallowed hard and dropped my hand, taking several steps back.

His eyes followed my movement and narrowed, but he couldn't hide the hurt he was feeling from my actions.

"Rumors have been greatly exaggerated." His smirk almost made me smile. I had thought I would never see it again in my lifetime. Instead, I brought my hands up to my hair and yanked. Giving a little yell.

"Now isn't the time for jokes, Ian Campbell." I tilted my head as I took him in. His usual stubble I had grown familiar with was now a full beard and his hair was shorter. One side looked like it had been shaved and was growing back. There was a nasty looking scar from what I could see towards the back of his head. "You are Ian, aren't you?" My tone had softened as I took him in. He still looked the same, but... not.

He nodded, then his eyes gave away a wince he tried to hide. "I am, darling."

Darling.

I spun around and paced to the door, then back again several times before stopping in front of him again. "How?" I lowered my voice from the yell that I hadn't been able to hold back. "How? Please tell me how this is possible? Because, Ian, you were not *alive* when you were here before. I don't understand what is happening and I am really, really not okay at the moment."

He stood up slowly as if he were having trouble getting to his feet and then, much like I had done when I first stood up, he swayed until he gained his balance. The whole time, he hadn't taken his eyes from mine.

"Isla and I were just discussing that while you were... sleeping."

I scoffed and crossed my arms defensively. "I wasn't sleeping. I passed out from the shock of seeing the man I loved walk through the door to his home after I thought he was gone forever."

With my words, he walked straight to me, ignoring my crossed arms, and took my face in his large hands, cupping my cheeks. His beautiful green eyes stared down at me with a raw tenderness that had me blinking rapidly. "I love you too, *mo ghràidh.*"

The fight left me and I uncrossed my arms to hold both of his wrists as we stared at each other. "Ian. How is this possible?" I whispered as he wiped away a tear with his thumb just to have another take its place immediately.

"Come, sit with me," He said gently as he took my hand and led me back to the soft brown leather sofa. As we sat, he gathered me close, placing his arm around my shoulder. His thumb swept over me as if he couldn't bear to not touch me.

"The day I fell from the balcony, there was a mixup at the hospital."

Isla scoffed. "You don't say?" It was then that I noticed she wasn't holding her usual tea cup. Instead, she had a glass filled with liquor in it. Her face looked ragged, like she hadn't slept in days.

He inclined his head. "There was another man brought in right about the same time I had been delivered by helicopter. He had been in a car accident. Flew through the window by all accounts. His head injury was similar enough to mine that apparently, a harried nurse got our charts mixed up. I was pronounced dead. And he was in a coma. For a month."

"Not that I'm not grateful that you didn't die that day. But that still doesn't explain how you were here parading as a ghost," I pointed out. He squeezed my shoulder and looked to Isla.

"I was worried about my sister and niece. Enough, I suppose, that I willed my... spirit to come here to keep watch over them. I knew what Elspeth had done to me and knew that she wouldn't stop until every last Campbell was gone."

"So you, what? Astroprojected yourself here? With no training or guidance?"

"It's a crazy thought, I know." He looked down at me and shook his head at my question. "I can't explain it. Much of my time in the coma was nothing but darkness."

"You said you could hear noises sometimes," I remembered.

"Yes. I didn't know what they were. I would come to the house and watch where I couldn't be seen. At the time, I truly thought I was a ghost." He looked at Isla with a sad look in his eyes. "I didn't want to scare Olivia."

"Of course," she murmured as she took a sip from her glass.

"Then you came. That first night you were here, and Elspeth targeted you immediately. I knew I needed to protect you, too. Only, you saw me that night. After that, you seemed to be a safe person to show myself to. The only person."

I nodded and leaned my head against his shoulder. He may be weak at the moment from being in a coma for a month, but his body hadn't diminished in that time. He was still broad and had the perfect shoulder to lean on.

"So, I tried my best to keep an eye on you and stop the witch from getting to you. Then I realized that you were trying to figure out how to stop her. I guessed that was why she was so determined to get rid of you. She had to have known that you were the first person to come around that could end her."

I shuddered at the memories of all that she had done in her quest to stop me. "It was awful."

"It was," he agreed.

"You guessed." Isla's slurred words came from the bottom of her glass as she drained it, then wiped her mouth with the back of her hand. I couldn't help but stare at the normally perfectly put together woman. I supposed she had a right to her own breakdown after finding out the brother she'd buried was still alive after a month. "You said, 'I guessed,' like you know it was for a different reason."

He smiled and then looked down at me. "That was my original thought, yes. But then once I got to know you, I realized that it wasn't because you were destined to end her reign of terror. She knew as soon as you stepped through the door of the Manor. All the ghosts did."

I held my breath and then whispered, "Knew what?"

"She knew that you were destined to be the next Lady of the Manor."

"Ian." My throat constricted, making it impossible to get out any other words.

"Elspeth knew I was still alive when I was taken away. Having you show up here was the final nail in her coffin, so to speak. If you were still alive once I came back, she would have to keep going for another generation. She'd already been trying to eradicate the Campbells for nearly two hundred years. I think even a vengeful ghost gets tired of fighting after a while."

Isla stood up and straightened her shoulders. "Well, I am going to go hug my daughter. Then I am going to have another drink before I go to bed and try to put this whole nightmare behind me." She looked at Ian and wiped a tear that was rolling down her cheek. "I am really glad that you are alive, brother. It means the world to me."

Ian squeezed my shoulder before removing his arm, then stood back up slowly. Once he was steady, he walked over to his sister and placed his arms around her. They stood there for several minutes holding each other and whispered soft words I couldn't hear. It was a touching moment that I was grateful to witness.

Finally, she stepped back with a shaky smile and looked around him to look at me. "Take care of my brother, okay?"

"I will. Goodnight, Isla," I murmured, and stood up to walk over to his side as she walked out of the room. Her footsteps could be heard walking through the marbled hall as the two of us stared up at each other.

"Now what?" I asked as I ran my eyes over his bearded chin and back up to his mossy green eyes that were looking down at me with love.

"Now, we go to bed."

Twenty-Nine

Ian was pretty winded by the time we made it up to my bedroom, even though he tried not to show it. I had told him that we should take the elevator, but he insisted on the stairs. I wanted to roll my eyes and tell him he didn't need to be strong all the time, but I figured he wouldn't appreciate it.

Together, we walked into the room and I watched as he shut and locked the door. I stood there nervously, not knowing what I should do.

"Do you want to take a shower?" I finally asked as he turned to face me, watching me with those eyes.

He shook his head very slowly from side to side. "I think that can wait until morning."

"Oh, okay." I looked around my room. "Would you rather go to your room? I'm sure it's a lot nicer than this one. Not that this isn't a lovely room. It is! I just figured, all your things are in there and your bed."

"Lacey?"

I stopped rambling and looked up at him. "Yes?"

"Shut up."

"Hey!" I said, indignant at his words.

His smile turned wicked, and he began to stalk toward me slowly. "You think that I'm going to sleep away from you?"

"Well, you're injured and..."

"I am healed. I may need to build my strength, but I had over a month of rest, darling. Do you think a little weakness is going to keep me from making love to my woman?" He stopped right in front of me, looking into my upturned face. His hands went to my waist. "All night?"

I swallowed as heat flooded me. Of course, I wanted him. There would never be a time that I wouldn't. "But..."

"I recall a time in the conservatory, that you rode me just fine." His smile was wicked as he pressed me back until the backs of my knees hit the side of the bed. I sat down with an oomph and his hands immediately went to my shirt, lifting it swiftly over my head.

"I missed these," he murmured as he cupped my breasts through my thin bra. "They feel so much better with these hands." He swiped his thumbs over my nipples, then pinched.

I gasped out loud and was suddenly out of excuses. "Okay," I moaned, and tilted my head back as he rolled them between his thumbs and forefingers. "But I saw you wince downstairs. I know your head hurts."

"I had to have surgery to remove the swelling on my brain. I was told I would likely have headaches for a while but that they would go away with time. Now, stop stalling. I need to be inside you, *mo ghràidh*."

Yes, I needed that too. I scooted backward on the bed and undid the button to my jeans. With his help, my shoes and socks, along with my jeans and underwear, were gone in no time, until I was left in nothing but my bra.

"I need to see you, too, Ian," I practically begged.

"What my lady wants." He smoothly removed the clothes he was wearing, likely something Isla had picked up for him to leave the hospital in, and climbed onto the bed with me. He gestured to my bra as he made himself comfortable with his head on the pillow I considered his. "Off."

"I don't remember you being so bossy when you were a ghost," I grumbled, but eagerly complied, sending the bra over the edge of the mattress to land somewhere among our other castoffs.

"Oh, darling." He chuckled as he held my hips while I climbed over him to straddle his hips. "You haven't even seen bossy yet."

I leaned down to finally bring our lips together. "Please, don't leave me again, Ian. I can't take it." I spoke softly, but earnestly, against his lips.

He brought his hand up to cup the back of my head and spoke with such finality that I couldn't help but believe every word. "Never again, darling, I swear it on my soul."

Our kiss turned fevered the second our lips connected fully. Even though I was on top of him, he was undoubtedly in full control. He guided my head in the position he wanted as he slanted our mouths together and slipped his tongue against mine, tasting me and groaning deep in his chest.

There was no need for foreplay. I didn't think either one of us could have handled waiting a second longer to connect fully. I was completely ready from the minute he looked at me with those smoldering eyes when he'd turned from locking the door.

I raised my hips until I felt his length part me and slide back and forth, my eyes almost rolling into the back of my head from the absolute pleasure his cock provided as it nudged against my entrance and then bumped against my clit with my movements. After several times of allowing me to glide along his length, he broke the kiss and gritted his teeth. His hands held my hips tightly, his fingertips digging into the flesh there.

"Enough. No more teasing me."

I gasped as he pressed me where I needed to go, allowing his cock to notch at my entrance and then with a swift move, he was bottoming out inside me fully. "I wasn't teasing you."

"I don't remember you being so argumentative." He grinned up at me, and with strength he shouldn't have had, he guided me by lifting my hips. It wasn't the same forceful way he had done before, but it showed me that he was still the same man he had always been.

With him leading the way, I used my thighs to raise and lower my hips until I couldn't anymore. But it was enough to rock on him, the pressure building into a crescendo. As I felt my whole body tighten up in preparation, my eyes popped open.

On a gasp, I choked out the words running through my mind. "I'm not anything,"

His wicked smile sent me over the edge as he pulled me tight against him and growled out, "Good."

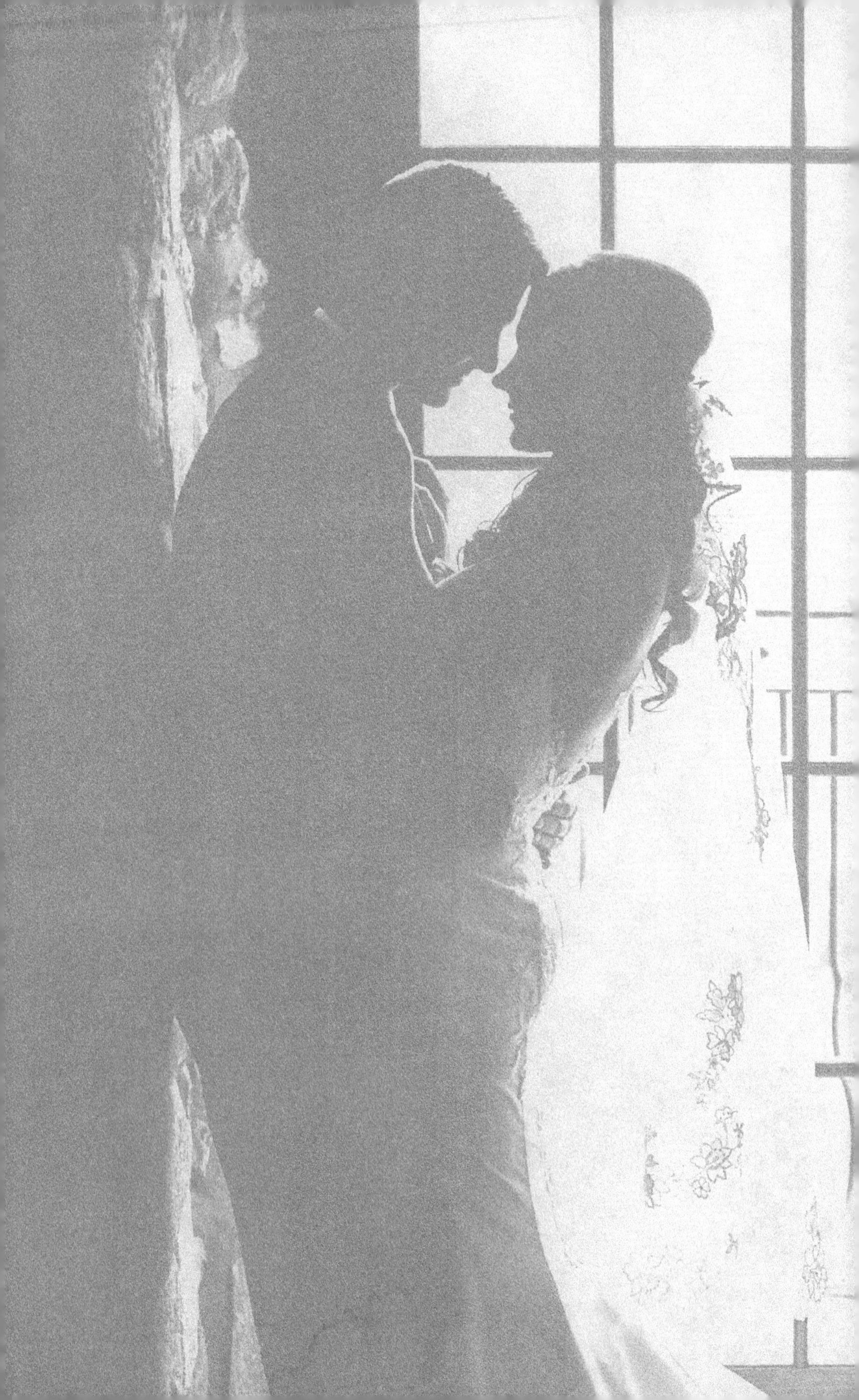

Epilogue

ONE YEAR LATER

I carefully balanced the tray with sandwiches and drinks and stepped down the front stairs, thanking Doogal for holding the door for me as he dipped inside the Manor to find his wife, who it turned out was the head housekeeper.

I walked along the path, following it around the house to the building towards the back. Once I got to the door, I paused and watched.

Ian was using a tool of some kind. I had no idea what it was called. I didn't know half of what he did to make the beautiful creations he did, but I certainly appreciated art when I saw it. He was etching an intricate design into what looked like a shelf that had drawers on one side and shelves on the other.

He paused what he was doing, always seeming to sense when I was near, and took off his safety glasses, setting them on the table in front of him. He dusted off his hands and then held out a hand for me in an invitation that I gladly accepted.

Once I reached him, he took the tray from me and allowed me to snuggle into his side, and I inhaled his scent. I was something I would never take for granted. I looked at the piece in front of us and asked him my burning question. "What is it?"

"That," he said as he ran a palm over my large belly. "Is our daughter's changing table."

I looked at it closer and realized the designs he was etching into it matched the same ones he had used on the head and footboards of the cradle he had made months ago. As soon as we knew I was pregnant, he had set aside all his orders that were waiting to be completed and shipped out to his customers and went right to work building the perfect cradle for our child.

"It's beautiful," I sniffled. He chuckled and pulled me closer. This far along in my pregnancy, he was used to my emotional outbursts, having watched me start crying over the most ridiculous things for the past several months. The other day while we were at the grocery store, he had to hold me as I cried in front of the row of diapers. Seeing the cute smiling babies had sent me into a fit of tears. He never allowed me to be embarrassed and would glower at anyone that looked at me strangely.

My anxiety wasn't gone, it didn't work that way. But with Ian at my side, it was easier to step out into the world. Not easy. Easier. He made me feel safe. He was like a shield between me and the rest of the world, and I knew he would always be there to protect me.

"I'm glad you like it," he said into my hair as he rubbed my back and waited patiently.

I leaned back and wiped my eyes. "I brought you lunch."

"It looks delicious."

"But you haven't even looked at it." I teased.

"It came from you. I know it will be perfect."

Every word he said to me had a way of making me melt inside. When my parents had arrived a couple weeks after he returned in a fit over being worried about me, he had a way of charming my parents, too. He had left with my father, and when they got back to the Manor after being gone for a couple hours, my dad was nothing but smiles. My mother was even easier to break. All he had to do was tell her what an amazing and beautiful woman she had raised, and she was nothing but smiles and was praising his charms to me. She practically threatened me when they were leaving for the airport with Doogal waiting in the car for them to say their goodbyes, that if I didn't marry 'that man' she would think I had lost my mind. There might have been a threat of disownment in there, too, but I knew she would never.

"You're too good to me," I said as I ran my fingers over his chest.

"Darling, you deserve the best. If I'm not giving that to you, then I don't deserve you."

He cut off my protests with a searing kiss that was enough to have my toes curling in my ballet shoes. The kiss had just started getting really good when my stomach let out a loud rumble. Ian pulled away with a chuckle and sat me down on his stool.

"I need to feed both my girls."

After cleaning his hands, my husband did just that.

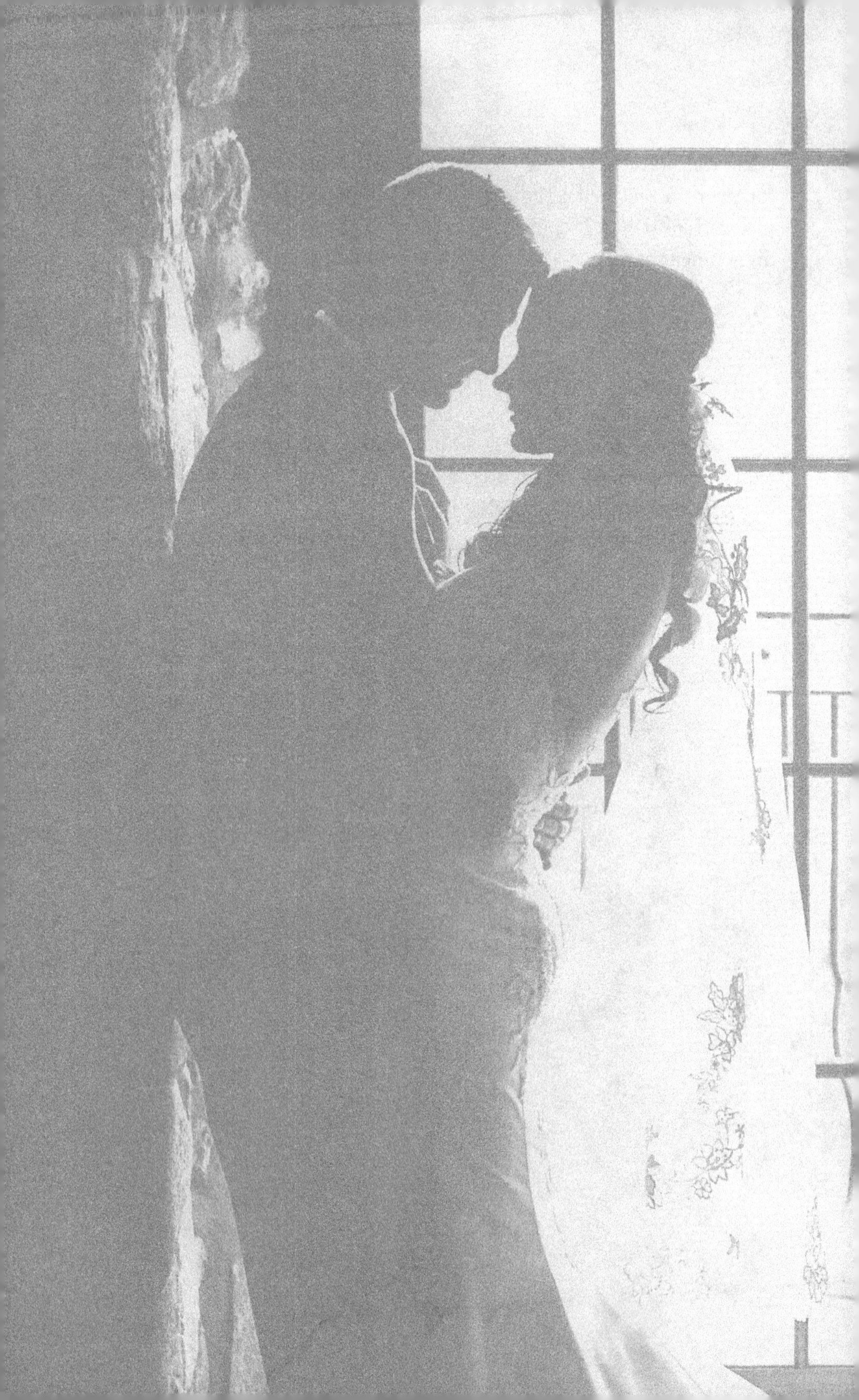

Epilogue

TEN YEARS LATER

Ian

I stepped quietly to the door of the nursery. My beautiful wife was sitting in the rocking chair, slowly rocking our sleeping nine-month-old. She was staring into space with a melancholy expression on her face. It was an expression I had seen on her many times in the last few days, ever since Moira's old nan passed away.

Lacey had gone to them shortly after she had spent that night on the cliffs, doing exactly what the old woman had instructed. She sat there with her, drinking tea and recounting every detail. After that day, she had become good friends with them and spent many of her days over the last eleven years, sitting by the fire, holding her hand. Losing her just a few days ago had hurt her deeply.

"Darling," I walked into the room and saw her blink, then turn her face up to look at mine. The smile that came over her face lit up my heart the way it always had. "Let me take Colleen."

She lifted our little girl up to me and as I took her into my arms, I held her close, inhaling her soft, baby fragrance. After placing a gentle kiss on her head, I laid her into her crib, making sure she was placed just so.

I took Lacey's hand and led her out of the room, closing the door softly as we left the nursery.

"Isla is coming tomorrow with Charles. Olivia is coming, too. She's excited to be able to visit before she starts Uni next week."

She leaned into me as we walked down the hall to our bedroom. "I'm so glad," she murmured. "I'm excited to see her, too. As will the children. They'll be so glad to be able to play with their cousins again." She smiled up at me. "I miss them, but I know Isla and Charles are happy in London."

Isla had met Charles while on holiday. He had fallen madly in love with my sister at first sight. Of course, she made him work hard to earn her. And he did. I couldn't have chosen a better husband or stepfather for my sister's family.

"We'll have to take them on a picnic to the ruins and let them play." I grunted because she was right. It was a favored place for them to explore. We just never let them go further toward the cliffs. None of us ever went there.

I pulled her into my arms as soon as we stepped into our room and closed the double doors with a soft snick. I grazed my nose over hers. "We need another."

She pulled back as far as I would let her, which was never far. "Another? You mean a child? Ian, Colleen is only nine months!" She laughed up at me, her bright eyes sparkling.

"Aye," I growled and leaned in to lick and nip her soft neck. "Another."

I never would have guessed that the love of my life would have been the one meant to break the curse surrounding my family for so long. If I could have saved her from all that she'd had to endure in her quest to save my family, I would have. But she was strong, stronger than she ever gave herself credit for. I would spend the rest of my life showing her how much I loved her.

Elspeth was long gone, and from now until forever, the Manor would be a place of light and laughter. All thanks to my lovely wife.

The End

Afterword

Thank you so much for reading Those Who Whisper!

TTW was something a little different and I hope you enjoyed it as much as I did while writing it. I loved trying to be spooky, it was about an evil spirit, after all. When I showed my favorite spooky scene to my teen, the only response I got was an "Uh huh," and they went right back to the video game I had interrupted. Well, then. My genius so under appreciated.

I'd love to keep in touch! Join my FaceBook reader group for fun, giveaways, and news on what I'm up to next!

RSullins Readers

For bonus content and to keep up to date on news and events join my newsletter!

RSullins newsletter signup

About the Author

R Sullins is a USA Today bestselling author, as well as an extremely avid reader. When she's not writing you can easily find her with a book in her hands.

She grew up in California but ended up living all around the United States once marrying her high school sweetheart, who just happened to be a soldier in the USArmy. Nothing is more important to her than her family.

She is a lover of fairies, tattoos, and coffee cups, has a vast collection of them all, and receives a glare from her teenager every time she brings home a new cup to squeeze into the cabinet.

You can find here in many places including here:
www.rsullins.com

Also by R Sullins

Paranormal Romances
Lovely Darkness

The first time she knew real happiness was when she found out that the man who raised her wasn't her real father.

She knew that there couldn't be monsters in the world that were any worse than the monster she had called 'daddy' for most of her life.

Then she stumbled into the world of demons.

The Demon King knew the second his fated mate had been brought into the world.

After living years too numerous to count, it meant little to him other than to keep him from living as he had.

He now belonged to only one female - and he would have to wait years for her to mature enough to matter.

How stupid and vain he had been to think that his fated wouldn't matter.

The very moment she entered his club he knew he had been wrong to ignore fate.

She was *his*.

And he was going to destroy everyone that hurt her, even if he had to burn the Earth realm to the ground.

Lovely Darkness

Completed story ARC
Hunter's Blood

Monsters exist.

They are all around us...

and I am the one they want the most.

They crave my blood.

The biggest secret of all?

I'm one of those monsters, too.

Hunter's Promise

I was **strong**, I was **deadly**, I was a **Hunter**

Until I became more.

There was an enemy with a plan to take over all vampirekind.

They were creating revenants that were smarter than they should be.

They listened, they followed directions, they killed.

They killed *me*.

Hunter's Forever

Someone from Crispin's human life reemerges

leaving us both reeling in shock.

If that wasn't enough-

My mate was *dying*,

and I was hiding a secret that would change our lives forever.

Suddenly,

the threat of someone dethroning all the leaders became very real.

We were in for the fight of our lives to save all vampirekind.

Begin with Hunter's Blood

CONTEMPORARY ROMANCE

A mature high school romance

Cry For Me

Paige

Loner

Outcast

Charity case

Orphan

I was all those things.

Years after my parents died, I was still being bullied, and it was all led by my cousins.

They hated me for years as children, and moving into their house didn't make them change their minds about me.

I was counting down the days until I could finally get away from every single person in this town.

Until there was one person I wasn't so sure I wanted to leave.

Reid

My life since age 7 revolved around football and what it would take for me to get into the NFL.

I didn't have time for girls or parties.

I had never been tempted by anything that could take my mind away from the sport.

Until I walked into my new school on my first day of senior year. One look was enough to change every plan I'd made for my future.

It wasn't long before we both realized that someone didn't like that we had found each other.

Cry For Me

FREE BOOK!
JOIN MY NEWSLETTER TO RECEIVE THIS FREE FULL-LENGTH BOOK
JARED IS A STANDALONE SET IN THE HUNTER SERIES UNIVERSE

Jared

The reluctant vampire...

This wasn't supposed to be my life

I never asked to become a *vampire*

Falling into this world of monsters turned out to be the best thing to happen to me.

The transition from human soldier to vampire sentinel was one of the easiest things I had ever done.

Now I was in for the fight of my life, convincing my *mate* to take a chance on me.

The mate in danger...

I couldn't return home no matter how much I missed it.

My mother forced me to leave for a reason.

There was an evil man after me, willing to kill anyone who got in his way.

Then a man walked through the door and set my soul on fire.

He said I was his *mate*.

I wanted to say yes.

But, how, when I had to save my mom from a killer?

The fight for their future...

I swore I would defeat all of her demons.

I wasn't going to let her go...ever.

I wanted to keep my mate safe, but what if I was the monster she needed saving from?

Download Jared and join my Newsletter now!

Printed in the USA
CPSIA information can be obtained
at www.ICGtesting.com
LVHW012133120823
755062LV00012B/830